LOVE OF THE WOLF

PACK LOYALTY
BOOK TWO

AMELIA SHAW

CHAPTER 1
TAMMY

The forest outside my window flashed past in a blur as we drove. The landscape was breathtaking this far outside the city, but I wasn't in the mood to take in the natural beauty that surrounded us.

Up front, Mick and Penny were chatting—no, *gossiping*. Their topic of conversation was fixed on one thing—the mysterious stranger Allara had eloped with a couple of weeks ago.

"I'm just saying, it's crazy she just ran off with him like that." Penny swivelled in her seat to catch my eye, and I gave her a half-hearted nod. That seemed to satisfy her, because she turned back and continued her discussion with Mick. "If any of my ex-boyfriends showed up, I wouldn't be taking them out on any dates, that's for sure."

Her long earrings swung from side to side as she talked. Penny was pretty, petite, and vivacious. A real firecracker. She'd had to fend off a guy or two from time to time.

"Nah," Mick said. I could see his profile, his lips drawn into a frown, in the side view mirror. "I saw the way he looked at her. It was deeper than some past fling, I'll bet."

"Allara said he dumped *her,*" Penny mused. "What?" She laughed, catching Mick's raised eyebrow look. "So, I eavesdropped a little! It was past midnight and there were no other customers in the diner. You can't tell me you wouldn't have done the same."

Mick just harrumphed and caught my eye in the mirror. "Check the map, will ya? This place must really be out in the sticks." We were in a remote area that provided no signal for a GPS.

Sighing, I opened the map and spread it over my knees, running my finger over the route we had marked out.

Of all the road trips I'd taken, this one had to be the weirdest.

First, the highway we were on was narrow and winding, with steep banks cut into the rock on either side of us. It was completely unmarked on the map itself, so we were basically following a series of crosses Reid had drawn for us and praying we were on the right track. We were in remote territory now, and if we got lost, nobody had any bars of reception on their cell phones to call for help. I couldn't ask Allara for advice, even if we had reception. Reid had invited us as a surprise for her, so she didn't know we were coming.

Secondly, Allara had disappeared from our lives, practically overnight. The only reason we knew she was all right was a short note she'd left for Mick, saying that she was fine and that she had to take care of some things at home. She said she'd only be gone a few days.

And finally, rather than appearing once again after a few days, we'd received an invitation from her hunky guy Reid to their wedding in Allara's hometown. Out here somewhere, in the middle of nowhere.

Only he didn't call it a wedding. He'd called it a *bonding ceremony.*

I had to admit, the wording intrigued me a little. I didn't have Allara pegged as the type to be into all that New Age, crystal healing stuff.

"Looks like we're on the right track," I said, glancing up at the road ahead. "We passed that cave thing on the left a couple miles back, right?"

"I think so," Penny said, sounding uncertain.

She and Mick resumed their debating and I tuned out, letting the sound of their voices wash over me as I went back to staring into space.

Truth be told, I hadn't known Allara very long. She was a good co-worker, and I loved working with her, but I'd always known the bar job was just a stopgap for her. A way to make ends meet, just like for me.

I was fresh out of college, having finally completed my last semester and had gained enough credits to earn my degree in child development. Allara and Mick had both surprised me by showing up at my graduation ceremony, which had been lovely.

All my friends and family wanted to know when I would start grad school to become a social worker. It had been my goal from the minute I'd started college, and they all knew it.

I blew them all off and kept my answers vague and non-committal. There would be time for all that later on. I was burned out and, if I were honest, I was fine where I was. Mixing drinks wasn't exactly the ideal way to spend my weekends, but it paid the bills.

Besides, it wasn't like I had anyone to spend my weekends *with.*

Not anymore.

I shook off the dark thoughts and focused on Allara. This was going to be *her* day, after all.

I knew the other two were curious to witness the mysterious bonding ceremony as well. Reid hadn't really described what would happen, but I got the sense that it wasn't like anything I'd seen before. I should be excited too.

But I couldn't shake off my misery so easily. It had sunk its claws into me a month ago, and it wasn't going away any time soon.

Time heals all things.

I wished I could believe it, but the advice I had heard from everyone around me was empty and meaningless. I was alone, and there was no disputing that fact. No way of inserting sunshine and rainbows into my life. The years stretched out ahead of me, barren as a desert.

No matter how I looked at the situation, the pain was still as deep as it had been that night.

The night that had changed everything and turned my whole world upside down.

Nothing made sense anymore. I didn't know when things would turn right side up again, when the pieces of my life would fit back together as they did before.

In my heart of hearts, I suspected they never would.

It was midday by the time we rolled up the narrow road and into Allara's hometown.

There were trucks parked on the side of the road, mud coating their wheel guards. We hadn't seen any signs of life since we turned off the freeway, so it was a relief to see evidence of civilization this deep into the woods.

The trees were just like Allara had described the few times she talked about home. Their trunks were thick; some stood wider than our car's width, and they were so tall I had to crane my neck up to see the treetops. Their branches were so high, it was like they held up the skies above us.

Mick parked on a small patch of grass littered with dirt bikes and other cars, and turned off the engine. Our arrival had not gone unnoticed. Several people were staring from outside a nearby house, and more than a few had stopped in their tracks.

Some of the kids were peering curiously, trying to get a better look at us. I waved at a small girl with long, braided hair, and she smiled at me before hiding her face in her mother's skirt.

"Well," Penny said, confident as ever. "I guess we should find out where to go. Wouldn't want to miss the fun."

With that, she opened her door and slid out the passenger side, landing daintily on her tiptoes so that her heels didn't sink into the grass.

I'd opted for simple flats for the occasion, as the invitation had suggested. The ground was firm beneath my feet, and as I inhaled, the first lungful of cool, forest air cleared my head, leaving me with a calmness that I hadn't felt in weeks.

"We're here for the… uh… bonding ceremony?" I heard Mick say to someone nearby.

"We have our invitation," Penny added, offering the stranger a card identical to the one I'd received. "Which way is the town hall, please?"

"Social hall," a man corrected her, sounding gruff. His eyes were narrowed, and he stood hunched over with his hands in his pockets. Another man wandered over and put a hand on the gruff man's arm. The first guy backed off immediately.

Huh. That was weird.

"Sorry about that," the second man addressed us with a warm smile, and we gravitated toward the friendly face. He shook each of our hands in turn as he spoke. "I'm Terry. The hall is right this way. I'll take you, as I was just heading there myself."

"Thanks." Penny smiled as we fell into step beside him. "We're not exactly from around here."

Terry threw back his head as he laughed uproariously. "No kidding! Everyone knows everyone else round here; that's just the way it is. Some don't take kindly to new faces, but they'll get over it soon enough."

"We're friends of Allara's," Mick explained. "From the city?"

Something flickered behind Terry's eyes, but other than that, his expression didn't change. "Sure, of course. Our Allara's always been one for adventure. Loves new experiences, all kinds of people. Here we are." He pointed to a building, slightly larger than the others surrounding it, with a low, pitched roof. "This is the social hall. The center of our little community."

We climbed the steps and found ourselves in a room with a vaulted ceiling made from roughly cut logs, some as large as tree trunks. The ceiling held a light fixture made from antlers, and the wooden benches were beautifully carved with leaping salmon, prowling mountain lions, and soaring bald eagles.

It was rustic, but beautiful. *Feels like home.*

Which was admittedly an odd feeling for me to have. I'd never been anywhere quite like this before. It certainly didn't look anything like what I'd always thought of as *home*.

The room was already packed. Practically every person in the village must have been in attendance.

With a shared look and an unspoken agreement, we chose a bench at the very back of the room and took our seats.

"Hey," Penny murmured, leaning in close to me. "Check out the eye candy."

I glanced over, following her sightline.

On the other side of the aisle were a group of youngish guys, sprawled out over the back benches and conversing lazily amongst themselves. Despite their casual demeanor, there was an alertness in the way they kept glancing over to the doors of the entrance that suggested they were keeping a close eye on the proceedings.

Almost like they're guarding the place.

But... from what?

This was a wedding, after all. Were they expecting someone to make a scene?

I didn't have time to wonder about what was going on, before

Penny's elbow caught me sharply in the side. "Dibs on the cutie!" she whispered, giggling.

Which one is the cutie?

The truth was, they were all as good-looking as each other. I couldn't work out which one in particular she meant.

Even though they were all seated, I could tell they were unusually tall. They were broad, too, the width of their frames causing their suit jackets to sit almost awkwardly across their shoulders.

All of them cut an impressive figure, with firm jawlines, and white teeth that complemented easy, perfect smiles. Country living certainly seemed to agree with these men.

For a brief, heart-stopping second, a pair of hazel eyes met mine.

My cheeks flushed with heat and I looked away quickly, my heart hammering in my chest. I furtively wiped my palms against my skirt and looked intently at the invitation that lay in my lap.

God, it's hot in here.

I told myself I must have been mistaken. It wasn't like any of them would be looking at me for any reason. They were probably staring at Penny, who was naturally attractive and vivacious, and I just happened to be in the way while they were scoping her out.

I was too nervous to check and see if I was right. So, I decided to keep my eyes to myself from now on. There were plenty of other things to hold my attention, after all. Up at the front, a group of musicians were performing a piece that involved a pair of huge drums. Although I couldn't see much from my position, I was intrigued by the braided hair of the women playing the music and the long, sweeping robes of the elderly man who stood at the front of the hall.

"There's a buffet after, right?" Mick mumbled to Penny, who *shushed* him as the music cut off abruptly and an eerie silence filled the room.

The double doors creaked open and a man entered through them, alone.

Reid... Allara's ex-boyfriend turned fiancé. The man who'd invited us here today in support of her.

I had a vague recollection of him from just a few brief moments when he'd stood in the doorway of our dim, smoky bar after Allara had punched that jerk who tried to hit on me and wouldn't take no for an answer. I'd only caught a few glimpses of Reid that night, but the two things that stuck out to me most were his height, as well as the rough, battered leather jacket he'd worn.

Just like those other guys across the aisle.

Just like the owner of the hazel eyes.

I forced my attention to remain on the groom—if that was what he was called, at a bonding ceremony. He was a lot more well-dressed than I remembered. His hair was combed, for one thing, and he was wearing slacks and a button up shirt that brought out the color of his eyes, which were just as piercing as those of the hazel-eyed guy.

Reid strode up the center aisle and came to a stop at the platform, just in front of the elderly man. The older guy looked like some sort of religious officiant, but I didn't recognize the denomination of his church. His robes didn't look like any that I'd seen before.

The drums picked up again, and soon the entire room was filled with the sound. There was buzzing through my feet and my body unconsciously began to move with the music. I didn't notice for several seconds, and when I did, I continued. Those around us were also swaying, as well as stamping their feet in time to the rhythm.

The doors opened once more, and Allara entered, accompanied by a few women who were also dressed to impress, but none of them could hold a candle to Allara.

My friend looked supremely radiant. Her long, dark hair was looped up into a complex pattern, fastened at the nape of her neck. She must have had someone else arrange her hair, because the Allara I knew would never have the patience to create that.

Her long dress was beautiful in its simplicity. The only decorative element was the embroidery that shimmered around the sleeves and hem of the garment.

As she passed us, I realized that the design emulated the foliage that surrounded this place. The forest was echoed in her headpiece, too; the delicate silver band was fitted with amber pieces. Their golden hue stood out against her dark hair, making her look regal.

Once she reached Reid, she turned to face him. The expression on his face at the sight of her was enough to send a shiver of envy all the way down my spine.

I sighed, wondering what it would feel like to have someone look at *me* that way.

It wasn't that I didn't feel happy for Allara. I did. Extremely happy. I knew she'd had a tough time, and it seemed as if she'd finally found her place in the world again. She was back where she belonged, with her people; her family.

And she had this gorgeous guy by her side, who clearly adored her. Anyone could tell that he would do absolutely anything for her.

I watched as they murmured their unusual vows to each other. They sounded arcane, almost mystical. Like nothing I'd heard before. He leaned in close to her to whisper something, and I watched her lips curve into a smile as she stared up at him with adoration.

I couldn't begrudge Allara her happiness.

And yet, there was a tiny part of me that ached with longing.

They were both equally gorgeous, and they looked utterly content together. Two halves of a perfect whole.

The beautiful ceremony unfolding in front of my eyes only exacerbated my feelings of loneliness.

I was sure to the depths of my being that no one would ever look at *me* that way. Never cradle my face like I was something precious and irreplaceable to him. Never kiss me like he couldn't get enough of my lips against his own. Hold me like there was nobody else in the room.

Allara's slender body curved to meet Reid's strong form. She was so lithe and feminine, her dress skimming over her body like water. I couldn't help but wonder what it would be like to look like her.

Next to women like Allara and Penny, I always felt so frumpy and ungainly. I knew I would never be petite like them. My weight had always bothered me, but in moments like this, it really came to the forefront.

Above all, I envied Allara because I could tell that she was totally secure. I envied her the security of Reid's love, even as I celebrated for her.

She knew the man she loved would never leave her or look at another woman. She knew that the love she felt was returned by her partner completely, and she had her whole community around her to celebrate this day.

It was a life I would never know, and I was humble enough to admit that it crushed me a little inside to acknowledge that fact.

Still, I held up my chin, smiling widely, and applauded with everyone else when Reid and Allara stood, their arms bound together, flushed and glowing with happiness.

It was a perfect day, and I wasn't going to let my private sorrow ruin it for anyone.

No way.

CHAPTER 2

JASON

A trio of folks I didn't know entered the social hall, led by Terry. Were they shifters, from another pack? After some deliberation, they sat across from us on the other side of the aisle. They were obviously invited guests and didn't seem threatening, so I barely looked at them, being more focused on the hall and my own pack, until Paul elbowed me in the side.

"Must be Allara's friends from the city," he hissed. "Don't cha think?"

Huh. Must be human, then.

We didn't get many ordinary humans up in our neck of the woods. Our settlement was deliberately hidden away, far from the main highways that cut across the state. Some of the children had barely seen outsiders before.

Humans weren't that interesting to me. They couldn't hike, run or climb like we could, and their senses were notoriously feeble. I hated the avalanche of noises and smells that greeted me any time I visited the city, and the way they gawked at us when they saw our eyes change always made me want to head straight back home, where I didn't feel so out of place.

But, just for a moment, I gave those city folk a brief look.

Not like there's anything better to look at right now, anyway.

The one on the end was a woman with a loud voice, bright lipstick and dangly earrings. Human as they came. She seemed to have spotted something she liked, though, over in this direction. She kept glancing over to us and giggling. To my annoyance, Eli and Paul didn't seem to mind this at *all*, judging by their identical smirks.

It was all I could do not to roll my eyes at their juvenile posturing.

Paul noticed my glowering face. "What?"

"Nothing," I muttered.

"She's hot, right?" he continued, indicating toward Dangly Earrings. Like I was going to miss the way his tongue was practically hanging out as he studied her. "D'you think I should go for it later?"

I shook my head, this time not hiding the eye roll. To avoid having to respond any further, I looked back to the humans and pretended to consider them.

Next to the loudmouthed chick was an older guy who didn't look quite as thrilled to be there as his friend did. I vaguely remembered hearing Reid talk about Allara's job as a bartender, and that she'd gotten to know the owner pretty well. From his description, this guy looked like he could fit the bill.

My attention turned to the woman sitting at the far end of the row.

She was dressed more soberly than the other woman, and her

curves were nicely plump. Her features were softer than those of her companions, a kind and gentle friendliness on her face as she glanced around the room. When her more garish friend nudged her, she looked across and caught my eye, and a jolt shot through my system.

Whoa. What the hell was that?

I almost glanced away from her, but something inside stopped me doing so.

Sweet. The word struck me out of nowhere as I continued to stare into her eyes, which had widened a little.

Did she feel this strange connection, too?

Around her face, her hair fell in loose, natural waves over her shoulders. The style, as well as the rich auburn color, was striking against her creamy pale skin.

Not my usual type at all. And yet, something about her arrested my attention and held it. I couldn't look away.

She folded her hands in her lap and stared down at them, breaking the moment.

I blinked hard a few times before slouching down in my seat. I tried to ignore the way my pulse picked up as a tingle of awareness sparked in every part of me.

It felt like my body had betrayed me with its reaction, and I didn't understand where it had stemmed from. I'd slept with more than a few women over the years. The corners of my mouth curled upwards as I thought of the women I'd bedded.

Confident shifter women, from packs out of state who'd been passing through our area to trade with us or to look for a mate. Hot women. Skinny, fit women.

In truth, not one of them were anything at all like the sweet human female sitting opposite me.

I had thought about bonding with a few of those ladies over the years. I genuinely liked a lot of them, and they liked me. But something had always held me back before I took that final step.

I could never put my finger on the reason. The humans would

probably call me a *lone wolf*. I had just figured I wasn't a commitment kind of guy.

I glanced at the woman again, surreptitiously this time, and told myself to pull it together. This was clearly a good girl; someone who would never look my way, let alone spend a night in my bed with no strings attached. I could already see that as plain as day.

As much as I was a commitment-phobe, she was a woman who would want it all from her partner. All, or nothing. This was a lady you wed; you didn't just bed her and move on.

The doors opened behind us and Reid strode through them, looking as uncomfortable in his fancy get-up as I felt in mine.

Every time I thought about bonding with someone—spending the rest of my life tied to another person and sharing *everything* with them—the whole idea seemed so crazy. It almost made me break out in hives.

Had things gone differently, it might have been Jaime up there right now about to bond with Allara, the Alpha of the pack.

And me as the proud Beta, standing by his side and supporting him every step of the way.

In the back of my mind, I knew it was a ridiculous thought. Allara would have never gone along with the bonding. Not with Reid already there in her heart.

And Jaime...

Well, the less I thought about *him* today, the better.

Allara herself came in soon after, and I watched the ceremony with a mixture of envy and sadness.

The envy confused me. Surely, I didn't want to be bonded to one woman, like Reid was about to do with Allara? Even if they both did look the happiest I'd ever seen them.

The sadness, on the other hand, was understandable.

Jaime had had a dream of being Alpha, and I'd been caught up in that dream right along with him. The dream had been snatched away in the blink of an eye, and I was still getting used to the new status quo.

But... maybe this is what's best for the pack.

Allara and Reid together, are strong, and that can only be good for us all, moving forward.

The sound of the drums carried me to my feet, and I hollered and stamped like everyone around me, but inside there was an empty, hollow feeling in my chest.

I wasn't quite sure what was causing it.

Without meaning to, I darted another glance over to our human visitors and caught an expression on the auburn-haired woman's face that seemed to mirror exactly what I was feeling.

On the surface, she looked supportive and happy. But there was something in her features that hinted the opposite. I sensed that she carried something sad deep inside her, just like I did. Something dark, like regret. Whatever it was, I could tell her emotions in that moment weren't so different from my own, despite the wide smile on her lips.

Hell, I need something to amuse me. Just so I can make it to the end of this confusing day.

I decided to make it my mission to find out just what that *something* bothering the mystery woman might be, and see if a little wolf company could put a more authentic smile on her face.

Maybe I was wrong, and she *would* consider a no-strings attached night of fun. The thought lifted my lips in my first genuine smile since Jaime had been defeated by Allara in the fight for Alpha supremacy of the pack.

CHAPTER 3
TAMMY

The reception was held on the lawn just behind the hall. It was a beautiful day. The decorations were perfectly set off by the sun glistening through the trees, and my heart warmed to see so many children making a dash for the open space after being cooped up inside for so long.

To the delight of Mick, the buffet table was laden with food and drink, and he immediately made a beeline for the victuals. Penny made a similar move for the wide lawn, predictably throwing herself into the thick of the social action without a second's hesitation.

I didn't know which one of them to follow. Getting a drink seemed like the smartest idea right now.

A strong one, preferably.

The people flooded out onto the grass, chattering, and laughing. The musicians came with them and struck up a square dance. Smaller children linked hands and persuaded some of the more enthusiastic adults to take turns swinging them around in a circle while they squealed with joy.

I smiled too, as I watched them all dance. The joy was infectious.

Allara and Reid came out of the building arm in arm, chuckling as they untangled the red velvet cloth that tied their arms and bound them together. Reid spun her around in his arms and tied the cloth around her waist, fastening it with a bow at the back and kissing her neck while she batted his hands away in mock protest, her eyes shining with pleasure.

I was so glad for my friend, who had obviously found her perfect man.

I found myself alone, sitting on the back porch of the social hall. I clutched my glass of white wine like it was a lifeboat and occupied myself with people-watching.

It was one of my favorite activities, especially at large social events like this one.

Reid was the life and soul among the kids, letting them clamber all over him. Now that his gruff exterior had dropped and he was back in his natural environment, I could see his playful spirit shining through.

He'd make a great partner for Allara. And maybe someday, a great father to their children.

I searched among the group for that captivating pair of hazel eyes from inside the hall, but they were nowhere to be found.

I didn't know whether to be relieved or disappointed.

The frisson of awareness that had shivered down my spine when I met his eyes, had been more than a little disconcerting.

A low, smooth voice traveled down to me, coming from somewhere above my left shoulder. "Don't fancy joining the party?"

I looked up slowly, my heart jumping in my chest when I realized to whom the voice belonged.

Hazel eyes. Black hair. Just the right amount of stubble.

Holy shit. He's actually speaking to me.

The man had undone his tie along with the top few buttons of his shirt, leaving a tantalizing glimpse of his chest on display. I wasn't sure whether he had purposefully sought to emphasize his impressive physique, but it was certainly working for me.

"Oh, I don't know this dance," I said carefully, pointing to the mass of partygoers, who were now weaving in and out of each other in pairs and spinning their dance partners around with enthusiasm. "Or any of the dances, to be honest. I'm happy to sit here and watch the fun."

To my shock, he took a seat next to me on the steps. He was a perfectly respectable distance away, but a shiver passed through me, nonetheless.

"Are you really happy to sit here and watch? That doesn't seem to be the case for your friend," the guy said, resting his elbows on his knees in a careless way and pointing in Penny's direction.

Sure enough, she was reveling in the music. Occasionally, she missed a step or trod on someone's foot, but she just laughed it off and carried on regardless.

"That's Penny," I said, feeling the need to explain. "She's extremely confident. She's just making it up as she goes along, by the looks of it."

"And you can't do that?" I turned to meet those devastating eyes. He was studying me with an intent expression that I couldn't quite read. "Make it up as you go along?"

"Definitely not," I mumbled, feeling inadequate as always. "Spontaneity isn't exactly my default setting."

"Maybe you just need to meet the right man to lead you in the steps." He flashed me a grin. God, his smile was so alluring. "Don't let life pass you by, Red. You never know what could be waiting for you right around the corner."

Red? My face heated as I registered the reference to my hair color. *How original.*

"I've tried the whole *man* thing, and it didn't exactly work out for me," I snapped. He looked askance at me, and I sighed. "Sorry. My faith in guys isn't exactly top tier right now."

He clicked his tongue and ran a hand through his hair. "So *that's* your damage," he drawled. "I was wondering. Back in there," he hooked a thumb over to the doors that led into the social hall. "You looked..."

He trailed off without finishing the statement. I decided to push further, feeling irritation rising in spite of myself. "Looked what?"

"I don't know... conflicted?" He stared at me, narrowing his eyes. "Now, maybe you just hate bonding ceremonies. But there's more to it than that, right? I could tell, just by looking at you."

I hope no one else could tell. Especially Allara and Reid.

I got to my feet and smoothed down my skirt, trying to rein in the hot rush of embarrassment and annoyance that flooded through me.

Why do all the hot ones have to be such assholes?

And why was he even talking to me, anyway? A guy like him could have any woman he wanted, most likely just by crooking his little finger or shooting them an inviting look. Women with gorgeous bodies, women who would laugh at his jokes, women who weren't too shy to get up and dance in front of strangers...

Women like Penny. Never women like me.

"I'm not a puzzle that you can just *pick apart* to satisfy your own amusement," I managed, after an awkward pause. "Allara's a good friend of mine and I'm thrilled that she and Reid are married... or at least, bonded."

He regarded me with a wry smile. "Same thing, in our world. And, I never said you weren't happy for your friend."

He hadn't moved from his position, comfortably sprawled out across the step. For some reason, the casual, arrogant display only served to inflame me further.

"I *am* happy for her," I said. I was telling the truth, after all. "I wanted to be here for her on her wedding day. End of story."

He didn't need to know anything more than that. I'd already given him too much ammo as it was.

And he definitely *doesn't need to know that he hit the nail right on the head without even trying. Bullseye. Fifty points to the arrogant jerk with the hypnotic eyes.*

"If you're referring to what just happened in there," he said slowly, "maybe you don't know her as well as you thought."

What does that even mean?

I stood and began to walk away, unwilling to entertain any more of his cryptic nonsense.

I had a half-formed plan to rescue Mick, who seemed to have gotten himself backed into the buffet table by a couple of angry husbands. I grimaced. Knowing Mick, he could have been hitting on any number of ladies.

Penny was still out there somewhere, flinging herself around the dance floor.

I tried to focus on my friends, managing to push the arrogant man out of my mind and assuming the caregiving role, which came naturally to me.

Dang, guess I'm the designated driver. Lucky for them I'm responsible.

Responsible enough to walk away from guys with loose ties and easy smiles, that's for sure.

"I didn't catch your name," I heard from somewhere behind me.

I looked over my shoulder. Him again.

I debated ignoring him, but innate courtesy won out. "It's Tammy."

His hazel eyes glittered, and in spite of my conflicted feelings, it was like the first time we locked eyes, all over again. My breath caught in my throat and my heart thundered.

"Jason," he countered. He didn't raise his voice at all, but it traveled over to me nonetheless, clear as a bell.

"Nice to meet you, Jason."

God, I'm losing my mind. Did I really say that, with a "come hither" huskiness in my voice?

The sooner I get out of here and back home to the city, the better.

~

JASON

Her words washed over me with the effect of lit gasoline. My blood ignited and the heat rolled right through me, from head to toe.

I watched Tammy walk away with a strange feeling in the pit of my stomach. I had a strong desire to catch her before she disappeared into the crowd, which was unusual. Women chased me, not the other way around.

I was so lost in my thoughts that I didn't notice Reid approach until he spoke.

"Hey." Reid shoved his hands in his pockets and looked at me, tilting his head. "It's almost time for the race up by the creek. You still coming, or what?"

I gave him a tight smile. "Wouldn't miss it, man."

He grinned back, a relieved look on his face, before strolling off, whistling to himself.

Reid and I had exchanged a few brief yet civil conversations over the last few days. Our awkwardness had a lot to do with Jaime's absence. As the pack's new Beta, Reid wanted to bring everyone into the fold, and make sure those previously closest to Jaime were happy.

And to keep an eye on us, of course.

Shifter packs were old-school when it came to allegiance. In our minds, one was either with us, or against us. There was no middle ground. No Switzerland.

Which put me in a bitch of a situation.

Many years ago, Reid and I had been like brothers. Back when everything had been simple. When we were kids, it didn't matter that Reid wasn't of our blood, that he might challenge one of us for control of the pack one day.

It was obvious—to those of us who would admit it to themselves, at least—that Reid was of strong blood. His size alone dictated he was at least born of a Beta wolf. More likely an Alpha.

But what kind of Alpha would give up his son? None of us knew.

Jaime was unstable; always had been. If he'd been allowed to lead, he would have walked the pack off the edge of a cliff if he thought it would further him in his quest for domination.

The way he ranted and raved about Reid was sickening. Allara, meanwhile, was nothing but an obstacle to him, to be used or destroyed as he saw fit. As Jaime's preferred second-in-command, I had found myself in a situation that was growing increasingly untenable, and yet I hadn't quite known how to extricate myself. The more Jaime seemed to lose it, the more I felt like I couldn't leave him, without somehow making the situation worse.

Allara had shown unexpected mercy toward Jaime, the day she let him go free. It was a mercy that he would not have shown her, had their roles been reversed.

We hadn't seen the last of him.

I also knew that, as Jaime's proposed Beta, I could easily have been left out in the cold along with him on the day he lost the challenge to become Alpha. I had been loyal to him for too long, and a wolf's loyalty was not easily broken. It would have been simpler in the eyes of everyone if I had been banished. Safer, too.

But Allara and Reid weren't like that. They would never banish one of their own, not without a good reason for doing so.

The only problem was, it was clear to everyone in the pack—and especially to me—that the two of them didn't trust me.

And what's a wolf without the trust of his Alpha?

I stared into the distance. The isolation sank into my bones as I watched the joy of the revelers shouting with laughter, celebrating the bonding of their Alpha with her mate. Without meaning to, Allara and Reid had doomed me to a purgatory I couldn't escape.

Even though it was a purgatory of my own making, through my own actions, it still hurt.

I was with my family, with the people I loved most in the world. And yet, I didn't belong. Not anymore.

I wanted to be part of the pack again. To be part of the future that the new Alpha was building, to gain back the trust of my former friend.

But this was my new fate. To exist on the fringe. Always on the outside, looking in.

I'd always been considered a bad boy as far as women were concerned. So, if I was gonna be cast as the pack lone wolf bad guy now, then so be it.

CHAPTER 4
TAMMY

It was early evening by the time I finally convinced Mick and Penn that it was time to head home.

"If we get lost in the dark, in those woods..." I trailed off, looking between the two of them imploringly. "There's no cell reception out here, no gas stations, nothing. We'll be stranded."

"So what? We'll stay here for the night!" Penny flung out her hands, staggering sideways, as Mick almost fell into the back seat of the vehicle.

They had obviously both imbibed rather generously. Very lucky for them that I hadn't indulged.

Penny had taken off her heels, and they dangled precariously from one manicured finger. "There's more than a few warm beds to hop into," she giggled, hiccupping. "If you catch my drift."

I struggled to shut out the hazel eyes that popped into my head at her words.

No! Forget about him, damn it.

Penny cackled when she caught sight of the look on my face. "You're blushing! Was it that guy you were talking to earlier? He was *delicious*. You got his number, right?"

"No point getting his number," I muttered. "No cell reception, remember?"

But she wasn't listening, already staring around at the crowd as if looking for one of the other sexy young men.

I turned away, willing my flaming cheeks to settle, and pretending to check on Mick. He was stretched out in the backseat of the sport utility vehicle. Every now and then he gave a light snore.

Well, at least that's one of them taken care of.

Penny's arm landed around my shoulders like a lead weight as she hung off me, listing a little to one side until I flung out my arm to steady us both.

"Hey, hey! *Tammy*, I said—"

"Nope," I cut Penny off, gently maneuvering her until she was safely situated in the front passenger seat. "I didn't get anyone's number."

Women like me don't ask for phone numbers from guys like him.

I realized with a jolt that there was no sign of my purse. I checked the vehicle footwells and the hatch, frantically retracing my steps in my head.

Damn it, I must have left it somewhere at the reception!

With a frustrated sigh, I turned and made my way back toward the social hall, picking up my pace when I heard the distant laughter of some of the villagers nearby. They sounded like they were on the move. If I could catch them, someone might have seen my purse lying around somewhere.

To my surprise, once I reached the lawn, the area was almost completely deserted. Only the whispering wind greeted me, stirring the leaves of the trees overhead.

Trying to ignore the sudden anxiety making my heart pound, I scouted around for my missing purse. My search came up empty.

Shit. Maybe I should just leave. It's going to get real dark soon.

Allara would mail it on to me, anyway. It contained nothing that I couldn't live without for a few days.

I was mulling over my options, staring into the tree line where the grass met the edge of the forest, when a strange light caught my attention.

One light became two, which then became four. I narrowed my eyes. There were about a half-dozen of them, all bobbing and weaving through the trees like fireflies.

What the hell?

Then I put two and two together. They were the lanterns from earlier. They had been unhooked from their poles and carried into the trees.

The party hadn't disappeared, after all. It was on the move, winding its way into the forest.

I glanced back the way I'd come. I should turn back. We had a long journey ahead of us. I shouldn't follow those lights. I shouldn't...

Penny and Mick are waiting for me. I have to drive them home. Come on, Tammy. It's time to leave. Walk away. Just turn around...

The hairs on the back of my neck stood up, and the flesh on my forearms rose with goosebumps.

Something was calling me, in that forest, and I had no idea what it was.

My feet carried me forward without my permission. I padded across the lawn, following the progress of the lights as they flickered like a beacon in amongst the dark foliage.

"I'm going to regret this." I spoke aloud, even though I was on my own. I couldn't seem to stop following.

What are they doing? Where are they going?

I kept a distance from the stragglers at the back of the group, using the sound of distant chatter and shouting from the party up ahead to guide me through the darkness.

I reasoned to myself that I was Allara's guest. This was her wedding celebration, wasn't it? It was her day, and we had been invited here, after all. I wanted to be there for her. She would not begrudge me my curiosity.

The trees were starting to thin, becoming smaller and more spaced out. I was nearing a small clearing. I kept a careful distance, wincing when a twig snapped under my heel and made a loud, cracking noise. Luckily, those nearest to me seemed to be too caught up in the excitement of whatever was happening to notice any noise I might have made.

A male voice floated over to me, carried in snatches by the wind, "The rules... simple... three laps from... to the ravine... no shortcuts, okay?"

I crept closer, daring to peek through the leaves to get a proper look at what was going on.

Most of the adults from the party were gathered around the perimeter of the clearing, clustered together in small groups. There was a gap at one end, and someone was dragging a tree branch through the dirt, drawing a rough line.

There were about ten people gathered at the center of the circle. I spotted Reid and Allara among them, along with Jason and a few of the other guys from earlier in the day. They formed a sort of huddle before breaking apart, whooping, and playfully shoving each other as they made their way over to the marked line.

Looks like they're about to run some kind of race. But why are they doing it all the way out here?

From where I was standing, the foliage seemed too thick to run through. The branches would snag their clothing and shred it.

I spotted Jason drop his suit jacket on the ground, pull his tie off his neck, and roll up his shirt sleeves.

Okay, so maybe him *losing his clothes wouldn't be such a bad thing.*

They all crouched down, like they were taking their marks or something.

Then, the strangest thing happened. In the fading light, it looked as if everyone's eyes flashed, swirling with an odd, silvery light.

And then those in the center of the circle... changed. Morphed into something non-human, right in front of my eyes.

I inhaled deeply, frozen to the spot with the shock of what I was witnessing.

Some humans remained around the outskirts of the huddle, but everyone in the center of the circle was gone. *Allara* was gone, and Reid. In their place stood a pack of enormous wolves.

The smallest of them could have comfortably looked me right in the face, even on all four paws. It was easily my height. The largest among them dwarfed the nearby spectators, with paws larger than dinner plates.

Oh, my God. They're wolf shifters.

And, suddenly, everything began to make sense.

Allara's sudden disappearance. This small community, so isolated, all the way out here in the middle of the forest. The strange ritual that I'd witnessed this afternoon, and the weird looks we got when we arrived here.

Jason's words rang through my head once again.

Maybe you don't know her as well as you thought.

Shit.

My fingers dug into the bark of a nearby tree, gripping it for dear life. I needed to grasp onto something real, and concrete, as everything I had ever believed about my work colleague and friend was turned on its head.

I let go of trying to make sense of my thoughts and focused on breathing, aiming to slow my pounding heart. The effort was futile.

Frantically, I tried to remember everything I'd learned about wolf shifters from movies and books.

They were much stronger than the average person. Faster, too.

All their senses were heightened. They had sharp instincts, and knew how to use them.

They're also fiercely territorial, and they don't like outsiders coming onto their turf.

Right. That would explain the cold shoulder we'd received on arrival. Lucky we weren't shifters ourselves, or else it could've gotten ugly, and fast.

A howl pierced through the air and I jerked, startled out of my reverie.

Several more joined in, until the air was filled with the sound. It should have been terrifying, and it was. But it was also hauntingly beautiful, almost like music, and I shivered in excitement as well as fear, as I listened.

How many humans had ever heard such a thing?

I heard a couple of human-sounding yells, and I realized the race had begun. The wolves leapt into a run with impossible speed, racing into the tree line and melting into the forest like shadows.

My thrill of excitement mixed with a new unease.

I shouldn't be here. This wasn't for human eyes.

I was about to turn away and try to fumble my way back through the trees, toward the relative safety of the village, when I froze. A new realization dawned on me.

A pack of superhuman wolves was roaming somewhere in these woods, and I was, quite possibly, their ideal prey.

Allara wouldn't eat me. I was certain of that. But I didn't know the others well enough to be sure. Would they all be as good and kind as my friend? Would... *Jason* retain his humanity, when he was roaming the forest in his wolf form?

I was about to blunder off blindly, in the dark. Straight into their path.

On one side of me, the clearing was filled with pack members in human form, talking and laughing amongst themselves. If I moved that way, they would soon discover me.

On the other side was the forest, were the wolves. If I started back the way I came, my shitty human senses would be no match for a stray wolf shifter.

They're at a wedding, Tammy! They're just having fun.

Still... what kind of fun did wolf shifters get up to, other than racing each other? Maybe the party earlier had just been the appetizer.

I swallowed.

Maybe I'm about to become dessert.

CHAPTER 5
TAMMY

A leaf rustled nearby and I closed my eyes, my heart hammering a mile a minute.

Allara wouldn't let them harm me. She'd always looked out for me. Every time a creep harassed us at the bar, she'd kicked them to the curb.

Allara can't protect you forever, said a voice inside my head. *You're all alone. You'll always be alone.*

Stop being such a baby, and learn to stand up for yourself.

I gritted my teeth, forcing myself to focus.

There was only one course of action. I had to walk into the clearing and show myself to the pack members who had remained behind in human form. Hopefully, they would take pity on me and take me back to the village.

I thought longingly of the SUV, where I had left Penny and Mick waiting, and cursed myself for my recklessness.

Serves you right, wandering into the forest so impulsively.

Okay, so, I had a plan. But unfortunately, my feet weren't getting the memo that it was time to move. They remained stubbornly rooted to the spot. Frustration and fear welled up in me once more, and I trembled. Just do it. Take a step forward and let them know you're here.

Thud.

The noise came from somewhere behind me. It was a heavy sound, like a weight being dropped onto the ground. Or...

Or the sound a gigantic paw might make when it landed on the floor of the forest. The sound of a predator advancing on its prey, slowly and deliberately, so that the prey didn't startle or run away.

My heart clenched and I almost whimpered out loud. Very, very slowly, I turned my head.

Out of the corner of my eye, I saw the wolf.

It was one of the bigger ones. Its shaggy fur was black, with a few patches of gray here and there. Its eyes were slivers of silver, and its gums were peeled back, teeth fully exposed in a silent snarl.

It must have caught my scent while racing the others.

But clearly, I was a more entertaining prospect.

My heart hammered in my chest, thudding with the speed of a high-performance engine, zinging adrenaline along my veins.

There was no point in running or shouting for help. I could tell from the look in its eye that this would all be over before anyone could reach me. Knowing my luck, I would only end up attracting more unwanted attention, anyway.

The massive wolf hunched down and backed up a few paces as it prepared to spring.

I closed my eyes and waited for the end.

Please God, let it be over fast.

But the death blow never came. Instead, I heard a growl, then a high whine and a loud thud, like the sound of a body hitting the side of a tree trunk.

Still paralyzed with fear, I inched one eye open to get a look at my surroundings.

My attacker was lying on his side, unmoving, next to a nearby tree.

What on earth...

Panting heavily, a second wolf stood where the downed creature had been a moment before. This one was also large, with dark fur.

I had escaped unscathed. For now.

Maybe this second wolf just didn't like to share his food.

Out of the frying pan and into the fire.

But my rescuer was... different from the other one.

His posture was upright, not crouched low. He didn't seem to be stalking me like the other one had, even though he was growling at me. A low, rumbling growl that I felt all the way through my chest, right down to my toes.

There was a sharp contrast between this growl and the one from the other wolf.

The first wolf had been ready to kill. I had read death in its eyes, and it had let out a snarl that was all vicious, blood-curdling aggression.

This one almost sounded like... a warning.

Like the wolf was pissed off at me, but didn't want to hurt me. In my head, I heard a human voice, more panicked than anything.

What the hell are you doing all the way out here by yourself? You're not safe!

I grimaced. Yep, I was *losing* my mind. Hearing voices in my head, that weren't my own.

The newcomer loped his way closer to me. I inhaled sharply. Fear prickled every one of my senses and I couldn't move a muscle. It was probably my imagination, but as I stared into his eyes, unable to look away... I swear I recognized him.

Jason?

And even stranger, I saw a flicker of recognition in return.

I moved backwards, flattening myself against the tree trunk as the wolf loomed over me. He had me pinned. He was so close I could feel the heat coming off his fur. It was a stark contrast to the chilly night air, and I shivered, fighting a sudden urge to lean in and rest my body against his warmth.

My reaction was as frightening to me as anything else in this moment.

And then, everything stopped.

The cold of the wind and roughness of the tree bark pressing into my back disappeared. The trees no longer rustled and the dull whining of the other wolf lying somewhere nearby faded into nothing.

The only thing I registered was the press of a very human body against mine. His eyes still glowed silver, before they faded a few seconds later into a familiar hazel color.

Jason was human once again, and his gaze was wide with astonishment.

I fell into those entrancing eyes headfirst and felt like I could never climb back out. He stared at me, conveying the same amazement that I felt as my body flooded with something I'd never felt before.

"Huh," Jason breathed. "Hey."

His face was so close to mine, our mouths were a few scant inches apart, and his bare torso pushed me insistently against the tree like he wasn't even aware of his own movements. His arms bracketed my head on either side, solid and strong. My gaze flickered to them, watching the tendons shift beneath his skin.

I swallowed hard. "Were you going to kill me?" I whispered.

"What?" He sounded dazed.

I felt like I had just been hit over the head with a sledgehammer. He sounded like he did, too.

What was happening between us?

"Your buddy almost tore out my throat," I managed. "Weren't you tempted?"

It was difficult to concentrate when we were so close, his body still pressed up against the full length of mine. To an outside observer, I wasn't sure if it looked like he was shielding me, or making love to me. His proximity was making my pulse race, nonetheless.

"No." Shock flashed across his features. "*No*, of course not. I—"

"Jason!"

Allara's voice from nearby was sharp, startling us both. He finally dropped his arms, allowing me to slide free of my confined position. Funny, there was a part of me that didn't want to step away from the warmth of his embrace. That thought sent heat racing to my cheeks, and I ducked my head, trying to regain some kind of equilibrium.

As he stepped backwards, I realized that he wasn't dressed.

Well, then.

My face heated even further and I averted my eyes from his body. I doubted it was humanly possible for my blush to intensify at this point.

"There you are." Allara burst through the undergrowth, breathing heavily and loosely buttoning up her shirt. Reid appeared just behind her, looking worried. "Oh my God, *Tammy!*" My name came out almost as a screech. She was obviously shocked to see me. "What are you doing here? I thought you'd left ages ago!"

"I..." Everyone turned to look at me, and the words dried up in my throat. I swallowed and tried again. "I lost my purse, and I saw... everyone heading out this way. I just automatically followed. I didn't know... I'm so sorry."

I wrapped my arms around my middle, trying to contain my nerves.

Allara's lovely features softened as she took me in. She put a hand on my arm and sighed deeply.

God, I must look like a complete mess right now.

"This is all my fault," she said, to my surprise. "I should've told you the truth about us. I thought it would be easier for everyone if I didn't. And now, I've put you in harm's way. *I'm* the one who should be sorry, Tammy."

"Are you hurt?" Reid murmured, stepping forward to stand by Allara's side.

"No," Jason said, before I could answer. "Paul just got a little carried away, that's all."

We all looked at Jason. He was sitting at the base of the tree he'd held me up against only moments before. The dazed look was still clouding his expression, and he couldn't quite meet anyone's eye.

"What happened?" Allara demanded, her voice authoritative. Reid slid an arm around her waist and she relaxed visibly, but her tone was clear, and the steel in her eyes didn't fade one bit.

So, she's in charge?

Hmm. Interesting.

"We'd just taken the corner next to... to the waterfall," Jason said, haltingly. "We were up ahead from some of the others, out on our own. I was on Paul's heels, hassling him a little, y'know? Trying to figure out a way to get ahead."

Allara nodded and Jason sighed, rubbing a hand over his face before continuing.

"Then I saw Paul turn, just a little. He lifted his head, scented the breeze, and immediately changed course." Jason swallowed. "Then I smelled... *her*."

He inclined his head at me, still refusing to meet my eyes. I forced myself not to shudder.

I wonder what I smell like to them. To him.

Attractive? In a sexual way? Or... like dinner?

"Paul took off, full tilt, through the forest," Jason said. "Like the devil was on his tail. You know how it gets sometimes. The mist descends... he was just acting on his instincts. But I knew she... I knew she wouldn't be safe, if he got to her. So, I took off after him."

A few feet away, someone moaned faintly.

Paul.

"Sure enough, he was about to spring," Jason said. For a split second, there was nothing but pure fury in his eyes. I was glad it didn't seem to be directed at me. "So, I jumped in the way before he had the chance to pin her. The end."

Allara was silent for a few moments, processing the information. She exchanged an unreadable glance with Reid, before turning to me.

"Tammy?" Her voice was gentle. "Did anything else happen?"

Yes. But I couldn't tell you what it was, that passed between me and Jason. Not for love nor money.

"No," I muttered. "That's... that's everything."

"I can give you guys a ride home," Reid said. "You've had quite a shock and you probably shouldn't be driving."

"Oh no, you don't need to do that—"

"They should stay," Jason cut in. I turned to him, surprised to find that he was staring straight at me. "Just for one night."

I'd fallen into his eyes again. Damn it. Nobody who spent enough time amongst these people could mistake them for normal humans. Jason's eyes smoldered even in the darkness. They gave off their own, almost hypnotically powerful, light.

"Of course," I heard myself say. "I couldn't possibly trouble you, Reid. It's your—"

I was about to say *wedding night,* but that wasn't quite right.

God, I didn't know what *was* right. I didn't have the first clue

"—the night of your bonding ceremony." I finished lamely. "It's a once in a lifetime thing, right? We'll be fine here until the morning. The others are probably asleep by now, anyway."

With any luck, Penny and Mick would remain passed out in the SUV until tomorrow.

"You're welcome to stay," Allara smiled. "It's the least we can do."

She linked her arm through mine as we set off back through the trees. The distant lights of the village soon began to twinkle through the undergrowth, and the knot in my chest eased at the prospect of a warm bed.

It had been one of the longest, most confusing days of my life, and I wanted nothing more than to put my head on a pillow and forget about it for a few, blissful hours.

"Thank you," I said to Allara, glancing behind me. I expected to see Reid or Jason following in our footsteps, but there was nothing but dark foliage.

"Don't be silly." Allara gave me a strange smile. "I'm happy to have you around a little longer." Her words were friendly, but she gazed off into the distance, as if she was lost in thought. "Besides... I'm not the only one."

My stomach flip-flopped as I considered the implication of her words. I knew who she meant, and I didn't know how to reply.

I wanted to tell her the truth about what had happened out in the woods. I knew I could trust her.

But what *was* the truth? I honestly didn't know. However, one thing was certain.

Tomorrow morning, I had to find Jason. We needed to talk.

CHAPTER 6
JASON

Allara walked off with Tammy, leaving Reid and me to pick up the half-conscious Paul and drag him back through the forest.

I was grateful to have something physical to do, to occupy my mind for at least a few minutes.

I was still gobsmacked over what had happened with Tammy—a *human* woman—and my brain needed time to process it.

In an unusually thoughtful gesture, Reid had tossed me some jeans and I was grateful for the cover as we made our way through the undergrowth on the way to the village. Wolf shifters didn't feel the cold like regular humans, sure, but it was nice to have *some* semblance of modesty when I was feeling so... unsteady.

I made sure not to manhandle Paul any more than necessary. The guy was still groaning from the hit he'd taken. And while I knew that he'd be fine by morning, I still felt bad. A bit. After all, I'd taken him down for a good reason. To protect...

Her.

He'd been about to attack Tammy, kill her most likely. If I hadn't been there, he would've finished her off in seconds.

I hadn't meant to slam him against the tree quite that hard, though. The poor guy actually bounced, before hitting the ground and staying there.

Reid was silent for the first few paces, which suited me fine. He was clearly deep in his own thoughts. After all, the night had taken an unexpected turn for everyone.

The adrenaline of my wolf form hadn't fully left me, and every leaf rustling and twig snapping underfoot increased my tension and agitation.

It was crazy. Tammy had left with Allara only moments earlier, but every inch of me wanted to abandon Paul and Reid and tear through the woods after her. I craved her with a ferocity that would be unsettling if I could think about it logically.

But that was impossible. I was on fire, and I couldn't do anything but burn.

"You know she'll probably head back to the city tomorrow."

It took me a minute to register that Reid had broken the silence. His voice was low and cautious, like he was talking to a wild animal or something.

In a way, he is.

"What?" I hefted Paul's arm, so that it was wrapped more securely around my shoulders. He was staggering like a drunkard, forcing me to steady him. It gave me a handy excuse to focus my attention on him instead of Reid.

"The human girl," Reid said.

"Her name's Tammy."

"Yes. I know that, Jason. I'm the one who invited them here." I could hear the almost-eye-roll in his tone. "I'm guessing they'll head back at first light. No reason for them to hang around here all day, after all."

I grunted. "What makes you say that?"

Reid shrugged his free shoulder. "Nothing."

We were silent for a few minutes. The trees were beginning to thin out, and I knew we were reaching the edge of the woods.

"Reid," the name tore out of me as I stood at the edge of the village and looked up at the dark shapes of the houses silhouetted against the starlit sky. "Just... just a minute."

Reid gave a nod and we stopped moving. Paul was pretty much a dead weight at this point, a dark shape hanging between us. Reid looked at me, unblinking, his expression imperceptible.

"When I threw Paul off the girl, I... I went to check on her." I swallowed, hearing my voice shake and I clenched my fists tight. "When we touched..."

"She's the one, isn't she?" Reid murmured. He wasn't looking at me anymore. His gaze was blank, staring in the direction of the tree-tops. I mirrored him. A large, pale moon hung in the sky, washing the grassy field with pale light. "Tammy. She's your Fated Mate."

My mouth dropped open at how perceptive he was. "How is it even possible?" My voice was hard as flint. I evaded answering his question directly, but I couldn't deny the truth of his words.

She's who I've been waiting for. All this time...

"She's a human," I said, more to myself than to Reid. "How can we be *destined* for each other?"

"It's not unheard of." Reid glanced at me, deep in thought. "All humans have shifter blood in them, you know that. For most of them, it stays dormant all their lives. Unless..."

Unless they are destined to mate with a shifter.

I couldn't argue with the genetic side of things. Tammy wasn't a shifter, and she never would be. But our children...

Our children will be like me.

Jesus, children. I'd only just met the woman, and suddenly I was picturing her having my pups? It was all happening so fast.

How was I so far removed from the person I was when I woke up this morning?

Reid seemed to catch onto my state of mind, because his expression grew consolatory. "I'll talk to Allara. I'm sure she'll convince Tammy to stay for a few days. This whole world—who and what we are, and how the Fated Mates thing works—is all new to her. She'll need some time to come around to the idea."

So will I.

Whenever I pictured bonding with someone, in the idle moments I'd entertained the prospect of settling down, the woman in my mind's eye had been... like me.

A wolf shifter. Strong, fast, confident. A little too sexy, maybe.

Someone who would fit in with the pack, who knew the way things worked with our kind. Someone I could share everything with. No secrets.

Someone who understood my world completely, because it was her world, too.

I turned to Reid, frowning. "How did you know?" I asked. "What you said, about Tammy." I paused for a moment, even her name on my lips sending a shiver down my spine. "It's like you knew what had happened in the forest before I said anything."

Reid's mouth twisted into a wry smile. "It was pretty obvious."

"Really?"

"Really," Reid echoed. "It was written all over you both. I've never seen you look like that before, man."

Ouch. If Reid knew, that meant *Allara* knew.

Which meant that I had lied to my Alpha's face.

As if reading my thoughts, Reid gave a loud bark of laughter. "Don't worry about it. You've just found your mate, Jason. Give yourself a break! Why do you think Allara wanted them to stay the night?"

I'll admit, I had entirely missed the subtext on that one. I'd been so wrapped up in my own shock over what happened, I hadn't realized how damn *obvious* I was.

Then something Reid had said penetrated, and my muscles relaxed a notch. *It was written all over you both.*

"So, you think she felt it, too? As strongly as me?"

Reid raised a brow. "That's how it works, with Fated Mates. I'm sure she did."

I parted ways with Reid with a murmur of thanks and headed home, taking a half-awake Paul the last few meters on my own. After depositing him on the sofa, I headed upstairs.

On the landing, I lingered for a moment outside the closed door of Kara's bedroom.

Call it a twin thing. Whatever it was, I was struck by a sudden urge to tell my sister everything that had happened tonight, and get her take on it all.

She hadn't come out to the forest to race. She'd been too tired, so she'd missed seeing the whole thing with Tammy.

She would probably give me a shove and tell me to get over myself. She'd say that some people waited their whole lives to meet their Fated Mate, and that many never got the chance.

You should count yourself lucky, idiot.

I couldn't decide whether that was the advice I wanted to hear right now.

So, in the end, I headed off to my own room, falling face-first onto my bed with a groan.

When sleep eventually found me, my dreams were riddled with the sound of running feet hitting the forest floor and feral snarls.

DESPITE THE LATE NIGHT, I woke before dawn, and lay staring up at the ceiling for a long while.

I knew that I had to see Tammy today and speak with her properly.

It was inevitable. And necessary.

Half of me – the wolf half – ached to be with her again. My human side told me that things were never straightforward, even in more favorable circumstances.

Regardless, whatever the day held for me, I would learn where my fate lay. Somewhere out there, just beyond my front door. Close enough to touch. Close enough to taste all its heady promise.

And, sooner or later, I would have to go and meet it.

CHAPTER 7

TAMMY

When I woke, I lay for a moment in the comfort of the warm bed I found myself in. I ran a hand over the soft quilt and basked in the morning sun that streamed in through the window.

The room Allara had found for me last night was in a house belonging to a woman called Rachel. It was simple but cozy, and much of the furniture looked handmade. A bunch of herbs were arranged in a jar on the bureau, and their scent filled the space with a soothing aroma.

I was so relaxed that it took a moment for my brain to catch up, and for yesterday and last night's events to come flooding back.

Jason found me in the forest. He rescued me. Why?

Maybe he didn't want his friend to have blood on his hands?

But one thing was certain. Something had happened between us when he held me against that tree.

The connection wasn't like anything I'd felt before, and the more I thought about it, the stranger the whole thing became.

The way he'd stared at me... Like, I was the only thing in the world he wanted to see.

I'd never been looked at that way before. It was the same way Reid had stared at Allara during their bonding ceremony.

Even now, as I sat in Rachel's small kitchen nursing a cup of coffee between my palms, I could run through every detail of the previous night in my mind with perfect clarity. The feel of Jason's skin pressed against mine, his hot breath on my face. The way his eyes had burned into mine so powerfully, even in the dim light of the forest. The warmth of his body, enticing me impossibly closer.

I felt an ache in my lower belly and between my legs, that I hadn't felt in a long while. But the connection was more than that; more than lust. I just didn't know *what* it was.

It was still too early to head back to the vehicle, but I couldn't sit still any longer. I wanted to be out in the fresh air again and enjoy the beauty of my surroundings while I had the chance.

I didn't know why, but something about this strange forest community cleared the cobwebs from all the dark corners of my brain and left me feeling lighter than I had felt in months.

I slipped out of the front door and shut it behind me as quietly as possible, so I didn't disturb my kind hostess. Outside, the grass underfoot was damp with dew, and drops of moisture clung to my shoes as I made my way outside.

There was a chill in the air this morning, and I wrapped my jacket tightly around my shoulders, taking in a few invigorating breaths of air.

It was so quiet here, so different from the bustle and noise of the city.

There wasn't another soul to be seen, which suited me just fine. I had always been content with my own company, and I wanted more time to process everything before I was faced with the entire...

Pack.

The word was so alien to me.

Allara had a pack. More than that, she seemed to call the shots. Last night, it had been clear that Reid and Jason deferred to her judgment. She had the final say over whether or not the three of us from the city stayed the night.

I glanced around at my surroundings, surprised to find that my feet had taken me back to the social hall. All closed up in the light of morning, it looked sleepier than it had yesterday.

My gaze snapped to the steps that led up to the wide entranceway.

"What's your name?" The voice belonged to a little girl of around seven, sitting neatly cross-legged on the top step, gazing at me with undisguised fascination. I thought I recognized her from the day before. She had been among the crowd of kids who'd waved at us so excitedly when we first arrived.

I wondered about shifter children. Did they shift into wolves, like the adults, or was that something that only happened at adolescence, or in adulthood? There was so much about Allara's life— about *Jason's* life—that I didn't know.

"I'm Tammy," I answered the girl, taking a seat on the bottom step and folding my hands in my lap. "What's your name?"

The girl blinked at me and twisted a long braid in her hair around her finger. "Lyra."

"That's pretty."

"Where are you from?" Lyra asked. "I haven't seen you before."

"I'm Allara's friend," I explained. "I used to work with her, when she lived in the city."

"The city," whispered Lyra, as if to herself. I smiled at the look of wonder in her eyes. "I've never been to the city before. Did Allara have her own pack there? Were you in it?"

I laughed as I caught onto her assumption. "Oh, no! We weren't in a pack." I paused before continuing. "I'm not like you, Lyra. I'm not a wolf shifter."

Lyra's eyes rounded. "Wow," she whispered. "That's what Sage said, but I didn't believe her!"

"Sage?" I tilted my head to the side, curious.

"My sister." Lyra bit her lip, frowning. "I've never met a regular human before. What's it like?"

I chuckled again, unable to stop myself. It had been a while since I'd been around kids of Lyra's age, and I'd forgotten how much I liked their forthrightness and honesty.

It's refreshing. Everyone else around here seems to speak in riddles.

"Being a human? Probably not as interesting as it is to be a shifter," I confessed, and watched her eyes light up with interest. "What's *that* like?"

"It's the best!" Lyra grinned widely, revealing two missing front teeth. "Well, I *guess*." She pouted a little bit. "I can't run fast yet or climb the tallest tree. Mom says it's because I'm too little."

"Well, I'm sure you could still beat me," I said, and watched her brighten at the idea.

I fervently hoped that she wouldn't take me up on it.

Getting into a foot race with a kid that would probably run rings around me? Not exactly number one on my agenda this morning.

Luckily, Lyra seemed to be more interested in quizzing me about life in the city than challenging me to a race.

Over the next half hour, I told her about my life. About the fancy drinks with the little umbrellas I made for bar patrons, the deep dish pizza from my favorite pizza place around the corner from my apartment, my upstairs neighbor's three noisy dogs that barked in the middle of the night for no reason.

I talked about the noise, and the traffic, and the hustle and bustle and general busy-ness of life in the city.

She listened to it all with astonishment, drinking in my words like she was committing them to memory.

"I much prefer the peace and quiet out here, though," I admitted, and she laughed.

"I don't," Lyra said. "I bet I would love noise and bustle best!"

I grinned at her, wondering if she would change her mind as she grew older.

For me, life here in the forest felt like an idyllic escape from all the chaos and misery I had left behind. But I could see that, for a kid like Lyra, the world beyond the forest probably seemed like an exotic fairytale.

I left out all the distinctly un-fairytale parts. She didn't need to know about them.

Let the kid believe that the world is good and kind, while she still can. I won't be the one to take that fantasy away from her.

I was halfway through explaining the concept of a karaoke bar when a shadow fell across the step I was sitting on, blocking the light from the early morning sun.

"Making friends?"

That voice had grown so distinct, so familiar to me in such a short span of time. It startled me, and I couldn't help but look up with trepidation. Had I imagined that moment last night? Was it all in my head?

"Lyra was just giving me a rundown of how things work around here," I said, shielding my face so that I could better make out Jason's form, backlit by the sun. My heart flipped. "She's been very—"

I turned back, but the little girl was nowhere to be seen. The spot where she'd been sitting only moments before was empty.

"Helpful," I finished, feeling confused.

"It isn't you." Jason extended his hand and I took it by instinct, letting him help me to my feet. The chaste touch shouldn't have affected me the way it did, but I couldn't help focusing on the warmth of his hand and the way it made my insides curl with pleasure.

This was the second time we had touched.

The real question here is... why am I keeping count?

I blinked and realized I was still holding onto him. I dropped his hand quickly and took a step back, my cheeks burning.

He's waiting for you to reply. What did he say, again? My sluggish brain finally clicked into gear.

"What isn't me?" I asked, blinking stupidly, and he chuckled.

Great, now he'll think I'm an idiot.

"She didn't leave because of you." Jason shoved his hands deep into his pockets and rocked back and forth on his heels. Despite his nonchalant posture, I could tell that he was holding something back. Something that made him uncomfortable, and faintly sad.

I couldn't say how I knew that, but it was as if I were tuned in to his emotions, almost as clearly as my own.

Then he added, "It's me, not you. If that's what you were wondering. I'm not exactly Mr. Popular around here these days."

"Why is that?" I asked softly.

He fixed me with an inscrutable look and ducked his head. We had to be around the same age, but there was a boyishness about him that was equal parts frustrating and deeply attractive.

He didn't answer my question, instead changing the topic swiftly. It didn't fool me, but I let it ride, for now.

"Were you satisfied?" Jason asked.

I released a shaky breath, my mind flashing to the night before.

His body had been so close against mine, the heat of him bleeding through my clothes. His arms encircling me, holding me steady. If the others hadn't arrived, I don't know what would've happened. The possibilities had seemed endless, and I had been unusually open to exploring them.

Satisfied? Nowhere near.

He gave me a crooked smile, his eyes glittering like he could read my thoughts.

Oh God, I hope mind-reading is not one of their super powers!

He cleared his throat. "I only meant... did Lyra answer all your questions about life here in the village?"

"Oh." Was I ever going to stop blushing around this guy? "Well...

no. I still have tons of questions," I confessed. "But we got kind of sidetracked talking about human stuff instead."

"Oh?"

"I guess those tiny cocktail umbrellas sound *really* exciting when you're seven years old." I scrunched up my face, and he laughed. "I do genuinely have more questions we didn't get around to, though. I mean, last night was a bit of a shock, all round, actually."

There. I'd said it. Kind of. At least I'd put the ball in his court in relation to whatever it was that had happened between us.

I stared challengingly at him, and he stared back. After a moment, he leaned in and offered me his elbow. The gesture was so unexpected and slightly old-fashioned I wanted to laugh, but instead, I bit my cheeks to hold in my amusement, and took his arm. The supple leather of his jacket was warm against my fingertips. Now he was wearing what I assumed were his usual clothes, he looked much more comfortable than he had in the more formal wear from yesterday.

"Come with me," he murmured.

"Where are we going?" I asked, picking up on his light, mischievous tone. It felt like we were playing hooky from school or something.

He smiled. "It's a surprise."

"I've had a few of those already in the last twenty-four hours," I muttered.

Unexpectedly, he laughed. "This is a good surprise. I promise. Trust me?"

Surprisingly, I did. My heart was a little lighter as he led me out of the village.

CHAPTER 8
TAMMY

"Okay, you can open your eyes now." Jason's voice was soft and lingering, so close that his lips barely missed brushing the shell of my ear.

I shivered at the sudden proximity and did as he said.

"Oh," I said, my mouth dropping open.

We were standing beside a small stream, on a bank carpeted with moss and long, trailing ferns. Toward the water's edge there were a few rocks scattered in amongst the foliage, creating the kind of natural spot I had only ever seen in movies before now. The sunlight dappled the water and the breeze ruffled my hair off my shoulders.

"It's so very beautiful," I said, sighing at the tranquil vision before me.

When I turned, Jason was watching me rather than the picturesque setting.

I looked away from his intense gaze, feeling suddenly self-conscious. "What?"

"Nothing," he said, but out of the corner of my eye I saw a wide smile break free.

WE SAT beside the water in silence, and I listened instead to the trickle of water, warbling birdsong, and the rustle of leaves above us. So different to the noises of the city, and so much more in tune with what my soul craved, deep down inside.

I just hadn't known that, until now.

I'd never been in a place as calming as this.

It was surprisingly comfortable being here with Jason, too, in spite of how little I knew him. It felt as if we'd known each other for many years, and we'd just returned to a favorite place only the two of us knew about.

I hadn't felt that close to anyone before.

Not even with...

No. We're not thinking about him. *Not today. Not ever.*

"No one else from the pack knows about this place," said Jason. His voice was low, confessional, like he was letting me in on a secret. Which, I suppose, he was.

"No one?"

He shook his head. "I haven't shown it to anyone else. It's a good thinking spot." He fixed me with one of his intent looks, his gaze piercing.

I felt honored that, for some reason, he'd decided to share his secret place with me. I wasn't quite sure why. It wasn't like gorgeous men were forever taking me to their secret hideouts, after all.

I suppressed a self-deprecating laugh. *So many gorgeous guys. I can hardly keep track of them all.*

"I won't tell. Promise." I smiled. "Thank you for sharing it with me."

He looked at me wonderingly for a long moment, until I was forced to drop my gaze. I fiddled a little with the sleeve of my jacket, at a loss for what to say.

"You do that a lot, huh?" he said.

"Do what?" I asked.

He replied slowly, carefully. I could hear a hint of curiosity in his tone. "Look away from me. Do I make you nervous?"

Very!

My heartbeat was strong but steady. I took a long, shuddering breath. I felt safe here, with Jason. "A little."

He chuckled. The timbre was loose and easy, strikingly melodic to my ears. "Don't be nervous. I won't bite."

Ha! Said the wolf to Little Red Riding Hood.

"Questions," I blurted out, my cheeks burning. I had to get the conversation back on track before this got out of hand. "I... I still have questions."

"Fire away." Resting a hand against the ground, he leaned back, tilting his head up to stare at the sky.

"Allara," I said. "I've noticed she seems to have the final say over things here. She called the shots last night. What's up with that?"

He shrugged. "Allara's our Alpha."

The way he said it was blunt. An open and shut case. *She's the Alpha.* Like there was nothing more to it.

I thought about that. "That means she's like... the leader around here, right?"

"It's more complicated than that," Jason said. "She looks out for us. She's responsible for the big pack decisions, though she takes counsel from others."

I heard the implication in his voice. "But?"

"*But.*" He threw me a crooked grin. "It runs more deeply than that. When a wolf shifter becomes the Alpha of a pack, the members of that pack are... beholden to the Alpha. You humans have your leaders, sure, but those bonds can be broken pretty easily, right?"

"Are you saying you *have* to do what Allara says?" I couldn't even imagine having that sort of power over someone else.

"In a way. My biology *wants* me to." Jason's mouth twisted. He looked like he was choosing his words carefully. "I could go against her wishes, but it would be overriding all my instincts to do so."

"Wow." I whistled. "That's crazy."

"Not if you're like us," he said, amused at my tone. "It's totally normal for wolf shifters. She has final say, but she's not a dictator. Reid's her Beta. He helps with decision-making, and tries to keep the rest of us in line. That sort of thing."

"That's kind of a crazy set-up for a marriage," I pointed out. "Running a pack together... I could see that getting in the way of a relationship."

He threw me an odd look. "Reid and Allara are Fated Mates, Tammy. They're meant to be together. It's literally in their blood. They're a... a perfect match, I guess you could call it. Brought together by Fate."

There was an odd undercurrent in his words, a tension that I couldn't read. I filed away that detail for now, deciding to examine it later. I had more pressing questions.

I was silent for a moment. "How do they know they're fated to be together?"

Now it was his turn to look abashed. He rubbed a hand over his mouth and turned his gaze toward the water, though I suspected he wasn't really looking at the stream.

"You just... know." His voice was low, so quiet I had to lean forward in order to hear him properly. "It's like... hearing your own name for the first time, coming out of the mouth of a stranger, and it just sounds so right on their tongue. Or solving a puzzle you didn't realize was a puzzle. One that you've been trying to solve your whole life, and then, suddenly everything falls into place and the answers are right in front of you."

"That sounds pretty good," I said faintly.

"It happens differently for each person," Jason continued. "For Reid and Allara, they've known each other forever. Since we were all kids. They just *fit*, you know? They were apart for a few years, sure, but they weren't *whole* until they found their way back to each other in the end."

I thought about the look on Allara's face the night Reid had turned up in the bar. She must have been so lonely, without her mate, for all those years.

"Yes," I said. "I can see that."

"Sometimes it's like a first-sight thing." Jason picked up a pebble and turned it over and over between finger and thumb. His hands were like the rest of him, tan and angular, with smooth, rounded fingernails. "*That* one's a shock to the system, or so I've heard." He caught my eye. "Sometimes, you know your partner by their scent. And sometimes—" He ran a hand through his hair, pushing it back off his forehead. "Sometimes you know you've found your Fated Mate the first time you touch."

My skin tingled at the memory of his hands on my body.

Don't be ridiculous, Tammy. You're not a wolf shifter! And you're not special enough to be anyone's Fated Mate.

What I felt yesterday was nothing more than late night excitement fueled by a near-death experience. It had to have been simply that, and nothing more.

"Feels like... like electricity, I guess." Jason gave a shaky laugh. "Tammy, come on. I don't need to explain to you. I think we both know what it feels like."

Ahh... what?

A flood of emotions crashed through me as he stared at me. He was acting as if I should know what he was talking about. But he couldn't be serious. I was no one's Fated Mate. It didn't make sense. What on earth was he thinking?

I don't know what Jason had been expecting from his freaking *soul mate*, but I couldn't be it.

"You can't mean…"

Jason grinned at me, as if happy I'd finally caught on. "That we're Fated Mates? Yep. Didn't you feel it?"

I blinked at him. "Well, I felt something. But… how is that even possible?" I rubbed at the spot between my eyes, where I could feel a stress headache developing. "I'm not like you, Jason. I'm not a shifter, I'm just…"

Me. Fat… average… human… me.

"It happens." Jason's brow creased as he looked me over. Strangely, his eyes were reflecting the same uncertainty. "It's rare, but it happens. I'm sorry, Tammy. This—" He gestured around us, to the forest, the trees. "—I know this isn't your world. You didn't ask for any of it. And I've gone and trapped you here with me."

I could have laughed in his face, but I bit my lip instead. It was crazy that a guy like him could feel bad on *my* behalf.

He's acting like he's Hades, leading me astray down into the Underworld.

Except he'd gotten it backwards. The story was all wrong.

"You could be wrong, you know," I said. "Maybe this is just some sort of… glitch?"

Because if what he was inferring was true, everyone would believe I was the one to trap him. This gorgeous, sexy, funny guy belonged to a world of danger and adventure.

Of sexy women and perfect bodies. I was nowhere near good enough for him, and I'd spend the rest of my life knowing he'd settled for me when he could have had so much more.

Someone better. Someone more exciting, more sexy… more everything.

And if he didn't already know that, well… I knew it was only a matter of time before he would come to the same realization.

But I couldn't seem to get up and leave. For better or worse, I wanted to stay close to Jason, for as long as I would be allowed.

CHAPTER 9

JASON

I sat on the rocks and watched her out of the corner of my eye. Her hair was truly gorgeous. As the sun rose, it blazed with color, curling over her chest and framing her ample cleavage.

My pulse raced at the sheer sight of her abundant curves and beautiful face. I wanted her badly, but I had to hold off for now. She was clearly disoriented from recent revelations and was probably struggling to adjust to all the new information I'd given her.

It wasn't typical for a human to end up in this situation. The last thing I wanted was to hurt her or make her feel uncomfortable.

It had been so long since I'd spoken with someone who wasn't a shifter.

One thing that kept confusing me was the way she shied away after every compliment I paid her, every glance between us that lingered a little too long.

At first, I thought it was her nerves showing, or some sense of modesty at the acknowledgment of our mutual attraction.

But I was beginning to think that she was simply *unused* to any attention.

I struggled to believe how anyone could fail to notice how gorgeous she was. She was not rail-thin and athletic, but that made her more unique. And far more attractive, in my eyes.

I had been struck like an arrow through the heart the very first time we locked eyes. I could tell that her reserved nature pushed her into the background, but she was the kind of soul who you glanced at once and then couldn't look away from.

She was lovely and, above all, I could tell that she was kind.

There were so many questions she wanted to ask. Every time I looked at her, I could see them shimmering behind her eyes.

Questions about Allara and Reid. Questions about why Lyra was so reluctant to remain in my presence.

Questions about the bond between us. How it worked, what it meant, and why it had happened.

She had every right to know the answers to all of those questions, and more. But she wasn't forcing them out of me, by any means. Instead, I was happy to talk.

I was used to sharing my innermost thoughts with those closest to me. I'd grown up with Kara's incessant poking and prodding, and Jaime would have never allowed us to hold information back from him.

It just wasn't the way a wolf pack operated. Having everyone up in your business sure got irritating at times, I could admit that much, but it was our way of life.

Tammy was different, though. She wasn't pushing me.

My heart raced when I thought of her simple acceptance of this fragile new thing between us, even if she seemed unsure about what it might actually mean for the two of us. I got the impression that maybe she saw herself as inferior in some way. Was that because she was human, and I was a shifter? In my mind, one wasn't better than the other. We were just different.

A desire grew in me, to protect her from hurt. Not only physical, but emotional hurt. I sensed that maybe she had been hurt badly in the past, and while I didn't know for sure, I wanted to help her let go of anything in her past that had made her feel bad about herself.

This was all new territory, though. I had no idea what to do, to protect her.

My new purpose—my innermost desire—was to keep her safe, and make her happy. I smiled to myself.

In her own way, by worrying about whether or not she was good enough, it seemed she wanted to protect me in return. I had been so focused on protecting *her*, it hadn't occurred to me that it could go both ways.

And to tell the truth, I wasn't sure what to do with that information.

～

I SAT WITH TAMMY, talking and laughing, until the sun rose fully in the sky and my stomach growled with hunger.

Half the morning had gone by without either of us noticing. *Huh.*

Time seemed to move differently when I was around her.

I held off on taking her back to the village, unwilling to face the rest of the pack. This place was a haven away from all the judging eyes and silent suspicion. We were in our own little bubble of bliss, and I was loathe to give it up before I had to.

Eventually, I was forced to concede that it was time to head back. I loved Tammy's crestfallen look when I mentioned it. Perhaps she felt the same way I did, and wanted to stay in our private little piece of heaven for as long as possible.

Reid waylaid me as soon as we reached the clearing outside the social hall.

Allara was at his shoulder and she drew Tammy over to her with a firm but gentle hand, fixing me with an unreadable look as she turned away.

Reid skipped the preamble. "So, I take it you told her she's your Fated Mate?" I nodded shortly. "I did. What's going on?"

"It's been decided that it's best if Tammy stays here with us." Reid crossed his arms over his chest. "For a few days, at least. I can't imagine that you'll have a problem with that."

I didn't, but I couldn't help but resent the intrusion on her behalf.

"Decided by who?"

"Allara. The pack."

Tammy wasn't a chess piece on a board, to be moved around as we saw fit. I wanted to get to know her properly, sure, but...

"It's up to *her*, Reid," I growled. "I'll go back to the city with her if I have to."

Reid snorted, probably at the mental image of me in the heart of the concrete jungle. Ugh.

Whatever. If Allara could stick it out for five whole years without her mate, then I could deal with it for as long as it took. Provided I could be with Tammy.

Something flickered behind Reid's eyes. Silver.

Uh oh.

I had to watch my step.

I wasn't scared of him. Strength-wise, I knew we were pretty evenly matched.

Why was I even thinking like that, anyway? We were on the same side now. And, even if it irritated me, at the end of the day, I recognized that he was only looking out for me.

Getting into a fight in the middle of the lawn with Reid was the last thing I wanted to do.

Like it or not, I knew I had more than myself to think about now.

I GAVE up on the idea of finding Tammy until later that day. The expression Allara had sent my way as they walked away said *back off* in about a dozen languages, including wolf shifter Alpha speak. So, I swung by my house with the vague intention of fixing a sandwich and quieting the rumbles of hunger in my belly.

As soon as I entered, however, I froze in my tracks.

"Jason?" Kara called from somewhere inside the house. "That you?"

Shit. Shit shit shit.

My first instinct was to run out the door, but it was pointless. There was no hiding from the visitor sitting in my kitchen. The scent —*her* scent—made me want to leave Idaho and never return.

Quit being dramatic, you pussy. Just get it over with.

With a deep sigh that was almost a growl, I padded toward the kitchen and stuck my head through the open door. Kara was hovering around the stove, making pancakes. And sitting at the dining table, a grin stretched across her face, was—

"Hello, Jason," Naomi purred. "Long time, no see."

My gut tightened but I forced myself to casually lean against the door frame. "Hey, Naomi. What's up?"

Naomi tapped her fingernails against the table and smiled, flicking her gaze up and down my body. "Not much. Just back for a visit, same as always."

"Sure." *Except nothing is the same, anymore.* I swallowed, heading over to the breakfast bar and pretending intense interest in the bowl of batter sitting on the counter.

Before I could stick my finger in it, Kara yanked it away. "Uh uh. Not for you."

Naomi smirked. "Oh, Jason's not very good at keeping his fingers away from things that don't belong to him, Kara."

Kara screwed up her face. "*Ew.* Gross."

Jesus, the woman is all class. This was going to get very awkward, very fast.

"Where have you been?" I asked, just to steer the conversation away from dangerous territory.

"Around," said Naomi, her eyes glittering as she fixed her gaze on me.

I frowned and looked away.

She was bad news. Bad, *bad* news.

Naomi and I went way back. She was part of the pack that lived over on the other side of the creek. And every spring, at the big pack meet-up that happened every year...

There had been a time I thought about sealing the deal with her. But I was just a kid then, too young and stupid to realize that she had a mean streak a mile wide and a habit of skipping town when her various misdeeds finally caught up with her.

She was hot, sure, but she was a mistake, and always had been. Like a forest fire, she was beautiful and bright, and consumed everything and everyone in her path.

"How long you sticking around?" I asked, trying to keep the tone of my voice level.

"Depends." Naomi looked up at me through her thick eyelashes. *Shit!*

Once upon a time, I might have said *on what?* I'd have matched her smirk with one of my own and probably fallen into bed with her to forget how lonely I was.

We'd danced this dance before, after all. Many times.

I folded my arms across my chest and stared at her with nothing more than annoyance bubbling inside me.

Did she come here to stir up trouble? Did she know about Tammy already?

I had a mate now, and a sensitive one at that. She wouldn't like one of my old bedmates hanging around. Hell, *I* didn't want my old bedmate hanging around.

We may not have had a bonding ceremony yet, but my wolf was

settled, for the first time in my life. My wolf and I were in perfect synch—completely happy with the choice Fate had made for me. Tammy was perfect, and even now, when we had only just parted, I ached to be near her once again.

Naomi, on the other hand, was just plain, old trouble.

I had to get out of there as soon as I could.

CHAPTER 10
TAMMY

I may not have fully wrapped my head around the way things were done around here, but I knew an ambush when I saw one.

Still, I allowed Allara to drag me away without putting up a fight. We had a lot to talk about, and if she was the Alpha around here, I imagined she'd be pretty busy most of the time.

"Good morning, was it?" Allara winked at me as we walked, and I shook my head with wry amusement at her cheery tone.

"I don't know what you're implying," I said, my voice light. "Jason and I talked, that's all."

"It's good to see you smile like that," Allara said, her eyes crinkling as she looked me over. "I haven't seen a smile on your face for a long time."

I shrugged, keeping my attention fixed on the trees overhead as we walked. "Something about this place makes me feel like smiling. As soon as I got here yesterday..."

It was true. I had felt like I was home, as soon as we pulled up in the car.

"I'll bet," Allara replied gently.

The path she led me down wound through the central group of houses, toward a slightly larger house with a wide porch that was set back from the others. She caught my look of surprise and smiled as she led me up the front steps.

"C'mon, you look like you could use something to eat."

Up until that moment, new emotions and nervousness had kept me preoccupied. But as soon as Allara mentioned food, I realized I was ravenous. Jason and I had skipped breakfast so he could show me his "surprise".

I followed her into the house and smiled at the coziness of the interior décor. "It's so homey here," I said, trailing after her into a rustic, sunlit kitchen. "So different from the city. In a good way, I mean."

"Well, we are out in the sticks." She laughed, rifling around in the cupboards for ingredients. "But I'm glad you approve! It can be peaceful, I guess, but my return was a bit of a culture shock."

"I'll bet."

"Tammy..." Allara had her back to me as she pulled out some pasta and various spices from the cupboards and the fridge. "I *am* glad you like it here. It's a relief that you do, honestly." She used her hip to shut a cupboard door and turned around to face me. "I'm not sure how to say this, but we're going to need you to stay with us. For a few days, at least."

Her tone was somber. Confusion struck me.

"Okay... But why?"

"Do you know what happened last night?" Allara tilted her head to one side, regarding me intently.

"Jason and I talked about it," I said. "He said something about Fate, bringing us together?" I chuckled a little and ran my hands through my hair. "Listen to me! It all sounds crazy, saying it out loud like that."

A soft smile crept over her face. "You really like him, huh?"

My cheeks heated. "I don't really know him, yet, but... I guess I do. He seems like a decent guy, and... well." I raised an eyebrow, trying for nonchalance. "They don't make 'em like that back in the city."

God, keep a lid on it! You only met the guy yesterday!

Allara grinned more widely. "So, you'll stay?"

"What about Mick and Penny?" I asked suddenly. "I was supposed to drive them home! I completely forgot all about them!"

How had I so completely forgotten my friends? *Because of the whole Fated Mates shock with Jason, that's why.*

"Oh, they left hours ago, while you were off in the woods with Jason." Allara set the pasta on the stove to boil. "I told them you would stay a while, and we'd drop you back to the city if and when you're ready."

If and when?

Fragrant smelling steam began to rise from the pot as Allara stirred. "I promise we'll take good care of you, Tammy," she added.

I thought about the big pile of nothing that waited for me back in the city and compared it to the excitement of everything that had happened here. There was no contest, really.

Screw it.

"Why not?" I said, my heart beating rapidly. "I'll stay." I couldn't even imagine leaving now. Not until everything with Jason was sorted out, one way or another.

A part of me still assumed he'd made a terrible mistake, and he would wake up to that, very soon.

~

TAMMY

Allara squealed with joy and leaned down to give me a tight hug. "Thank *God*, that's a relief." She returned to her cooking, looking like a weight had been lifted off her shoulders.

I folded my hands in front of me and fiddled with the bracelet that encircled my wrist. "So, what's the deal with Jason?"

"What do you mean?" Allara asked. Her voice was suddenly noncommittal, deliberately casual.

"What's he like?"

Allara shrugged. "I know his sister, Kara, better than I know him."

"You guys must have all grown up together," I pressed. Something about the way she was dancing around the subject struck me as... *odd.* "C'mon, Allara. It's me, Tammy!"

"We did grow up together." Allara folded a dish towel, smoothing it flat. She began twisting it round and round in her hands, lost in thought. "We were inseparable as children, actually. The four of us—Reid, Jason, Kara and me."

I heard the wistful sadness in her voice. "So, what happened?"

Allara opened her mouth, then closed it again. She seemed unsure of what to say.

"Don't say nothing happened." I held up a hand to forestall her. "I sense a sadness in Jason; a regret that he tries to hide. And I'm sensing the same thing now, with you. And if he's my Fated Mate, then I deserve to know. Don't I?"

Allara sighed heavily. "When I came back here," she said. Her voice was hushed, a stark contrast to her usual confident tone. "Reid *brought* me back. At first, I didn't want to return."

In halting tones, she told me about the night Reid found her in the bar and let her know her dad had been sick. Dying.

Poor Allara. I couldn't imagine how alone she must have felt.

Just as I suspected, there was more to the story. I listened to the tale that unfolded and it made me shiver. This was a world of rage and retribution, of bloody battles and territorial conquests. Allara's fate could have been so different if things had gone the other way.

"So. This Jaime," I said, once Allara had finished her story. "Where is he now?"

"I don't know," Allara said simply. "Reid's pretty sure we haven't seen the last of him, though. And I agree. A wolf doesn't just give up like that. And a crazy wolf like Jaime will only stop once he's dead."

"What's any of this got to do with Jason?" I asked.

"Jason?" Allara blinked, surprised. "Didn't I mention that part? Jason was Jaime's best friend. He would have been his Beta, if Jaime had defeated me and become Alpha."

My stomach dropped. "What?"

As soon as I think I have a handle on this place, something comes along and knocks me off my feet once again.

So *that* was why Lyra disappeared as soon as Jason had shown up. That was why Jason always seemed to be on the fringe of things, like he was on the outside looking in, even though this place and its people were all he'd ever known.

"Ever since the day I banished Jaime, Jason's kinda... kept to himself," Allara explained. "There were those who believe I should have cast out the both of them." Her face hardened. "But that's not the kind of Alpha I want to be, Tammy. Where do I draw the line? Do I banish everyone who might have sided with Jaime if he had become Alpha?"

I shook my head, helpless. "I don't know."

I'm just glad I don't have to make those kinds of decisions.

"I refuse to punish someone who hasn't committed a crime against this pack," Allara said. "And, whatever happened in the past, Jason is loyal to his family. I trust Kara, so I trust Jason."

I wavered, thinking about every encounter I'd had with him. Behind the bravado, there was an underlay of something warm. Gentle, even. Maybe behind those glittering hazel eyes, there was a kind heart.

He must have felt so alone, for a long time.

"Jason was Jaime's right-hand man for years." Allara slid a steaming bowl of pasta in front of me, and I inhaled the delicious aromas gratefully. "If Jaime were Alpha right now, Jason would be the pack's Beta. It just didn't shake out that way."

Wow, that was rough. To have an expectation of your life going a certain way, only to be left out in the cold through circumstances beyond your control.

I can relate.

Pushing my dark thoughts aside, I took a bite of pasta and chewed, thinking hard. "Was Jason on board with Jaime's plans for the pack? Would he have gone along with everything Jaime had planned?"

Bloodshed, brutality and domination. Whatever cultural differences lay between us, there were certain lines I wasn't willing to cross.

Allara gave a deep sigh, taking a seat opposite me with her own bowl. "Who can say? It's complicated. Our kind... I'm afraid that it's in our nature to be loyal to those closest to us. Even if they bring us nothing but pain."

I stared out into the forest, feeling a sharp ache in my chest.

Maybe humans and wolf shifters weren't so different, after all. And that wasn't necessarily a good thing.

I SPENT the afternoon wandering aimlessly around the village. The conversation with Allara had cleared up a lot for me, but I was left with the realization that once again, I was standing on the outside of this world looking in.

My thoughts were interrupted by a crowd of small children led by Lyra, who waylaid me on the gravel path in the center of the village.

"Hello, Tammy!" Lyra bounced up to me, taking my hand like we were old friends. My heart warmed as I let her drag me forward. "Come and meet everyone!"

In due course, introductions were made. I met Lyra's older sister, Sage, a girl of about ten who seemed to have adopted a teenage eye-rolling habit a couple of years early. JJ and Ethan were identical twins with identical tooth gaps. Eva, a shy little thing with long plaits who spoke in a soft, whispering voice, and Teddy, who had even more questions for me than Lyra.

Before I knew it, I was sitting with them all in a circle in the long grass and quizzing them on everything I could think of.

If there was one thing I'd learned from college, it was that kids were like tiny sponges. They soaked up everything at this age, and it was clear that these children in particular were hungry for knowledge of the outside world.

"Don't you have class?" I asked, puzzled.

In truth, I didn't see how they could go to an ordinary school out in the middle of nowhere, like this.

"We used to have Miss Jackson," Teddy informed me solemnly. "But she left a couple of months ago. She lives with another pack now, but she promised to visit. Sometimes one of the other adults teaches us stuff, but..." He shrugged, and it was obvious from their responses that these children had been allowed a rather ad hoc approach to education.

"We do have a schoolhouse, though," Lyra piped up. "Wanna see?"

"Absolutely!"

TRUE TO THE children's word, it was clear that the schoolhouse hadn't seen regular use in some time.

With effort, I managed to get the doors open. A cursory peek around at all the facilities told me that this place could do with a serious update. The windowsills were full of cobwebs and one of the lightbulbs was busted.

A few rows of desks were set up in a small semi-circle, with a large teacher's desk in front of a blackboard at the other end of the room. There were a few plant pots in a row on the windowsill and the walls were covered with craft displays and other projects.

All in all, it was old-school, but serviceable. Underneath all the dust, I saw a bright, happy place in my mind's eye.

While I was here, I reasoned, I might as well make myself useful.

With that thought in mind, I set about putting the room to rights. I explored a little, and found a spare bulb in a box under the teacher's desk. I showed the kids how to sweep away the cobwebs from the windowsills and desks with a feather duster.

I got so absorbed with my self-appointed task, I didn't even register the knocking until JJ tugged on my sleeve and pointed in the direction of the open door.

"Rachel!" Lyra rushed over, jumping into the arms of a woman I remembered from yesterday's ceremony. *Rachel.* This must be the woman whose house I stayed in last night. She hadn't been home when Allara dropped me there and showed me up to my room. "I made a new friend!"

Rachel laughed, hugging the girl tightly before setting her down and looking up at me. Her eyes were kind and I returned her smile easily.

"You must be Tammy," she said, extending a hand and grasping mine warmly. "You stayed in my guest room last night."

"Yes." I scanned my memory frantically, hoping I'd left the room in a decent state. "Thank you so much! It was lovely."

"Don't look so worried," Rachel chuckled. "It was a pleasure! I've had far messier house guests, believe me."

I must have looked puzzled because she patted my arm a couple of times as if to reassure me. "I raised Reid, from when he was about this high." Gently, she pulled Teddy toward her and ruffled his hair. Teddy giggled and tried to duck. "And believe me, when Reid hit teenagerhood... well, there's nothing like a teenage boy to wreak havoc." She kissed the top of Teddy's head and the boy wrinkled up his face.

"*Rachel!* I'm not little anymore!" Teddy looked up at me, eyes wide. "I'm almost *nine*."

"Wow," I said, nodding to show how impressed I was. "Almost into double digits!"

Apparently satisfied with my response, Teddy ran off to join in the game the others were playing. They had abandoned the feather dusters in favor of chasing each other around the desks and shouting with laughter.

I smiled, watching them for a moment.

"Yes, Reid was borderline feral at that age," Rachel murmured, smiling to herself. "He, Allara, Jason... all of them."

"Jason?" I struggled to keep the interest out of my voice. Judging by the twinkle in her eye, something told me that I hadn't succeeded.

"Oh, yes," Rachel said. "They were the best of friends, once upon a time."

Huh.

Things seemed to have cooled off considerably since then. Still, I guess kids weren't kids forever. Life got complicated sometimes. I should know.

"Do you have kids?" Rachel asked suddenly.

I shook my head. "No. I've always wanted them, but I never found the right guy."

I paused as I realized how insensitive that sounded. This woman had just told me she'd raised Reid. Did that mean she'd done it all by herself?

"I'm so sorry," I bit my lip. "That came out wrong. I didn't mean..."

"Darling," Rachel put a hand on my shoulder, gently silencing me. "It's perfectly all right. It's wonderful if you can find a partner to do these things with. But it's clear to me that you're more than capable of going it alone, if you choose."

"Really?"

"Sure!" Rachel smiled. "You kept this bunch occupied for most of the afternoon, didn't you? These are shifter children, Tammy, with a whole bunch of pent-up energy that never seems to wane. That's no mean feat, to hold their focus so long. How do you think I found you? I was wondering why it had gotten so quiet around town all of a sudden."

I burst into laughter, and she joined in.

Strange. I actually feel happy.

All the pain I'd felt over the past few months... maybe it hid something deeper.

I didn't know how, but it was like I belonged here. Almost like...

I blinked a couple of times as the thoughts hit, hardly daring to believe it. It seemed impossible, ridiculous. And yet...

It's like I've finally arrived home.

CHAPTER II
JASON

After making my excuses to Kara and Naomi, I ducked out of the house and spent the afternoon deep in the forest, after first shifting into my wolf form.

I'm not running away. I'm just clearing my head.

Who was I kidding? I was totally running away.

Being in wolf form felt as exhilarating as ever. The other night had been a maelstrom of confusion and panic, and it felt great to leave all that stuff behind for a few hours. The thud of my paws through the undergrowth, and nothing to focus on but the sounds of nature around me...

Naomi, Tammy, Allara, Reid, Jaime...

I needed the space to stop thinking about any of them and just enjoy the rush that always came with shifting.

I pounded across the forest floor, the trees flashing past on either side of me in a blur of greenery.

Eventually, I knew I'd have to return and face the music.

I was finding it increasingly difficult to ignore the magnetic pull somewhere deep inside my chest. The pull toward Tammy. My mate.

I trusted that Allara would look after her friend, but to be a lone human in the midst of a wolf pack would be unsettling. I had to get back, and check that she was okay.

By the time I returned, dusk had settled over the village. The pack had built up a large bonfire in the middle of the lawn, and several rough wooden benches were scattered around it.

I spotted Tammy sitting at the edge of the circle and made a beeline for her. "Hey."

She looked up, and her eyes softened visibly at the sight of me. "Hello."

She shuffled up a little to make room for me on the bench and I sat beside her. We watched the flames flickering in silence for a minute or two.

"I'm staying," she said.

It sounded like a challenge. I caught her gaze and watched the fire dance in her eyes. "I'm glad."

More silence. I was very aware of our close proximity. This was the nearest we'd been to each other since...

Since it happened.

"How was your first full day here?" I asked, and her face lit up with a wide smile.

God, she's beautiful.

"Really good," she said, her voice full of happiness. "Tons of new people," she giggled. "Mostly the kids, but I'll get around to everyone else soon enough, I'm sure."

She spotted Rachel, who sat across from us, and waved. Rachel waved back, smiling broadly at Tammy. To my surprise, the older woman's smile even extended to me.

My gaze snapped to the fire to hide my shock. I had become so used to my outcast status, I'd forgotten what acceptance felt like.

"You like kids?" I asked, swallowing the lump that had lodged itself in my throat.

She nodded. "My degree was in childcare, so..."

I waited for her to elaborate, but she didn't. Instead she just shrugged, and trailed off to nothing. I sensed there was more to the story, but something told me to leave it alone for now.

"Maybe you could help with the schooling situation round here," I said. "The kids are all kinda running wild at the moment."

I winced. *And that's an understatement.*

She let out a knowing chuckle. "Yeah, I gathered that. They're sweet kids, though."

"They'd rather play in the woods than learn their times tables," I grumbled, and ducked my head at the sound of her answering laughter.

"And I'm sure you were *so* well behaved at their age." Her white teeth nibbled at her plump lower lip, and an ember of something hot flickered between us.

"Sure, I was," I drawled, picking up a stick off the ground and poking at the edge of the bonfire with it. "Nah, you're right. Jeez, I remember when Reid and I—" I broke off, running a hand through my hair. "It was a long time ago now."

Curiosity was written all over her face, but she didn't question me further.

I decided to change the subject. "What's it like for a human? The whole..." I waved a hand between the two of us. *Soul bond.*

I didn't know why I couldn't say the words out loud to her, all of a sudden. It felt too... intimate. Especially out here, surrounded by everyone else watching us.

Jesus. Harden up!

Tammy's expression grew reflective. "I don't know. Like nothing I've ever felt before. What's it like for a wolf shifter?"

"I told you." I grinned at her, appreciating the way the color rose in her cheeks. "It's pure electricity."

"Why me?" she asked. I watched her eyebrows draw together as she gazed at me. "You could take your pick, Jason. So many young, strong and attractive shifter women for you to bond with."

So, I was right. She *was* worrying about the fact she wasn't a shifter.

"The bond doesn't work like that, Tammy. You don't pick and choose for yourself. Fate chooses for us."

"What if Fate chose wrong this time?"

I opened my mouth to reply, but snapped it shut again. I couldn't deny it, the thought had been weighing on my mind, too. Not that Fate had chosen the wrong mate for me, but that I wouldn't be able to protect her properly, living here among a pack of wolf shifters. I couldn't bear the thought of something happening to Tammy, and all because I happened to live in an environment that might not be safe for a human.

How could a human live among us? *Would* it be safe for her here, in the long run?

But she was already surprising me. Various pack members were greeting her like she was an old friend, and she'd clearly won Rachel over with ease.

Most of all, when it came to the kids, she'd clearly hit her stride. The pack was in desperate need of a tutor for the younger children and Tammy would be perfect, especially if she'd studied childcare at college.

Maybe this can work out after all.

I was getting way ahead of myself. Just because she fit in with the pack didn't mean all our problems would be solved.

She's not like you. You can't ask a woman you barely know—a human, at that— to give up her whole life for you.

"For my kind..." I swallowed, thinking about how to explain.

"This bond is a pull like no other. Undeniable. Irresistible. And it only happens once. And for me, it was you, Tammy." I edged my hand close to hers, brushing our fingers together. "Only you."

~

For our pack, a bonfire signified one thing. Being together. A family.

Food, booze, music, stories, and conversation. Everything flowed freely between everyone on bonfire nights. The air was thick with smoke and laughter, and even the kids were allowed to stay up late to listen to the elders tell stories about the old times.

It was the best kind of night.

Usually.

Tonight, I couldn't appreciate any of it. I was so distracted, I barely even noticed when the festivities finally wound to an end and I was staring vacantly into the dying embers of the fire.

Beside me, Tammy was chatting easily to Terry.

I was half paying attention to their conversation, but the bulk of my attention was focused on the lock of hair that fell loosely across Tammy's shoulder. It shone like copper in the firelight. I wanted to run it between my finger and thumb to see if it was as soft as it looked.

"Jason?"

I looked up to discover Terry had already left, and Tammy was staring at me with a concerned expression.

"Are you okay?" she murmured.

In a movement that seemed almost unconscious, her hand slid over mine, bringing me back to the present. Grounding me.

In answer, I slid my other hand into her hair, tilted her head up, and kissed her.

She gasped with surprise and I took the opportunity to flick my tongue against hers, groaning at the sensation and the taste. She tasted like strawberries and her skin was fire-warmed and as soft as silk to the touch.

We broke apart after a moment and I rested my forehead against hers, panting. "Does that answer your question?"

She melted into me, and our mouths met again, over and over. It wasn't long until I was completely lost in her.

CHAPTER 12
TAMMY

I felt weightless in Jason's arms, like floating on a cloud.

His skin was hot to the touch, his muscles firm under my hands. Pleasure pulsed through me when he buried his face in my neck and his hand slid down the front of my dress.

His thumb grazed one of my nipples and I let out a wanton moan, forgetting we were still out in the open, where anyone could see us.

The fire pit was long deserted.

His arms are so strong and steady. I could stay here forever, just like this.

Soon, though, my desire for him started coiling sharp and hot in my stomach. I needed more.

I shifted into his lap and gazed up at him imploringly, hoping he'd decipher what I couldn't bring myself to say out loud.

He did, letting out a feral growl before hoisting me up like my weight was nothing to him, manhandling me until he had me in a bridal carry.

I wrapped my arms around his neck. He dropped kisses on my parted lips as he carried me into the darkness. I wondered vaguely where he was taking me, but I couldn't bring myself to care, as long as it was somewhere away from prying eyes.

It was dark in the forest, which suited me just fine. The low light made everything so much more potent. His scent was everywhere, and I could feel every one of his ragged breaths against my lips. The pulse of his heart thundered in my head, drowning out my own.

It was like I couldn't tell where one of us ended and the other one began.

He lay me down in the soft moss and guided my hands up under his shirt, my eyes fluttering shut at the brush of his bare skin against my palms.

"Tammy," he rumbled. "I need you."

I whimpered at his words and pulled at his shirt, needing to get closer.

He reared back for a moment, stripping himself of his clothes, pulling his shirt from his shoulders and pushing his jeans to the ground.

My breath caught in my throat at the beauty unveiled to me.

I had seen him naked the night we connected, but now I had the time and the focus to see him properly, with no one else around to judge if my gaze lingered too long on his beautiful strong body.

I reached out to him, and as he lay back down between my waiting thighs, I arched up, capturing his mouth in another searing kiss.

I hadn't been with a man since... well.

It was crazy to be out here like this, about to have sex under the stars, but everything about it felt perfect.

We'd been dancing around each other from the moment we locked eyes at the bonding ceremony. It was always going to end like this, I could see that now.

I still couldn't believe that someone as amazing as Jason would want someone like me.

But it was clear how much he *did* want me from the way he licked his way down my neck and held me firmly against him, allowing me to feel the thickness of his cock against my belly. I groaned, grinding against him.

What was also clear was that Jason knew exactly what he was doing. His moves, his touches, were practiced and skillful.

How many other women had he done this with? Was I the fifth girl this month he'd taken out into the forest to ravish? Or the tenth? I had no way of knowing, and though I needed to know, something in me shut that line of thought down.

Consider it tomorrow. Tonight, just focus on the here and now. On his talented fingers slipping under my skirt, sliding his fingers against my clit while his mouth found a sweet spot just behind my ear that made my eyes roll back in my head when he explored there.

Eventually, I couldn't stand the torment anymore. I needed him inside me. I panted the words into his ear, my toes curling at his answering groan.

He drove into me without warning, then froze, and we both gasped.

"Oh, God," he said in a deep, husky voice. "I'm trying to not hurt you..."

As he began to move slowly, rocking inside me, it was obvious he was holding himself back.

"Fuck me," I whispered. "Like I know you want to. I can take it. Fuck me hard, Jason."

His head dropped onto my shoulder, his teeth scraping my throat.

Then he did exactly as I asked, driving into me over and over again. The pleasure was incredible, making me cry out and grab for him until my core tightened around him.

I was close and didn't have the time to warn him. I bit into his shoulder and moaned, shaking as the climax crashed over me. Wave after wave of bliss rippled through my body, leaving me boneless and exhausted and clinging to the gorgeous man above me.

He followed soon after, his eyes rippling with a glint of silver as he came. Aftershock pulsed through me as I reveled in the moment.

Then the thoughts started crowding back in. He'd clearly been with a lot of women.

But... how many *human* women? Was I the first? I hoped so.

I pressed my face into his shoulder and felt my satisfied smile curve against his skin.

Guess I'll have to wait to find out.

~

JASON

It didn't take much persuading to get Tammy to come and stay with me that night. Kara was off somewhere, so we had the house to ourselves.

Once we got inside and I realized we were alone and could take our time, I almost regretted my impulsive actions earlier.

Almost.

Taking Tammy like that, in the middle of the forest... it hadn't exactly been part of my game plan. I was usually the smooth type, wining and dining a woman before undressing her piece by piece. I liked to savor my conquests.

But this was different. There had been no calculation on my part, only a wild need that seemed to be mirrored in Tammy, and it drove the both of us crazy.

She brushed past me into the house, looking around the dark

hallway with interest. I could smell myself all over her and the wolf inside me growled with satisfaction.

She's finally mine. And tomorrow, everyone's gonna know it.

The rational side of me knew I should think about the logistics of what that actually meant, but right now I couldn't feel anything but relief. I had finally satisfied my instincts, cleared my head enough that I could start to think about other things.

She pressed up against my shoulder, standing on her tiptoes to kiss my cheek. The gesture was unusually chaste, given what we'd just done in the woods.

Okay. *Tomorrow* I would start to think about other things.

She looped her arms around my neck, and I walked her upstairs, listening to her giggle with happiness in my heart. It felt good to hear her laugh. The sound was a world away from the withdrawn, reserved woman I'd met just a couple of days ago.

I ran my hands over her generous curves, appreciating her softness. She was still flushed, warm to the touch, and it made me almost ready to go again.

However, by the way her eyelids were drooping, it wasn't going to happen again tonight.

Sure enough, once she was in my bed, she was out like a light, molding herself into my side like she belonged there.

And the crazy part was... she did.

That's another first to add to my list. I don't think I've ever had a female stay overnight in this house before.

For some reason, I couldn't keep the grin off my face.

I wrapped my arms around Tammy, and fell into a deep sleep almost the minute I closed my eyes.

CHAPTER 13
JASON

When I woke, I felt totally replenished in a way I hadn't felt in possibly forever. I opened my eyes, stretching my arms above my head. The window was open, and the white curtains billowed out, filling the room with fresh air.

Outside, I could hear faint voices. The community was stirring, ready to start the day.

I wasn't, however. Not yet. I just wanted to stay in this little cocoon for a while longer.

I rolled over, flinging out my arm, finding only a vacant pillow. The space next to me was empty, only rumpled sheets beside me now. I sat up.

"Tammy?" I called.

She edged into the room. A dressing gown was wrapped tightly around her form, and she looked strangely shy. I frowned.

That's weird. I thought she enjoyed last night. Did I read something wrong?

"Come back to bed?" I pulled the covers back invitingly.

Her cheeks flushed and she bit her lip, adjusting the tie on her robe. She sat on the edge of the mattress, taking care to avoid sitting on my feet.

"You could try getting under the comforter," I joked, and she smiled back hesitantly.

I couldn't figure out her sudden reluctance, but I decided to just charge ahead anyway.

I flung back the covers, my feet hitting the floor. "Breakfast, then?"

If you can't beat 'em, join em, right?

A warm smile crept across her face. One hand stroked the material of her robe, back and forth, like she had a nervous tic. "Sure."

I bit my lip, looking her up and down once I realized that the robe was mine. Something about seeing her wearing my clothes excited me in a new and unfamiliar way.

Her gaze met mine. She'd caught me looking. I grinned at her, unrepentant.

"I don't have any clothes with me," she explained, looking sheepish. "I wasn't counting on staying so long."

Huh. I hadn't thought about that.

After some digging through my closet, I managed to find an old flannel shirt and some sweats that fit her well enough. She made me leave the room while she changed, which only heightened my feelings of puzzlement.

What's happening? Is this a brush off?

Feeling disheartened, I wandered downstairs and set about making us some French toast. It was the only fancy breakfast thing I could make, and *dammit,* I wanted to impress her, at least a bit.

Maybe this had only been a bit of fun for her. To be with a wolf shifter, the novelty of it... Maybe, now that she'd had me, she'd be on her way?

Take them to bed, then leave them. That was my style, right? There would be a certain irony in having my own moves thrown back at me.

Especially if it was done by the only woman I'd ever really wanted to stay.

I heard her coming down the stairs and shook off my morose musings, forcing a smile onto my face. She took her plate gratefully and we curled up on the sofa together.

"What's your morning usually look like around here?" Tammy asked.

I shrugged one shoulder. "Depends. When it's lumber season, I'm out in the woods for days on end. Sometimes I go hunting."

We lived a rural life around here. I couldn't sugarcoat it for her, it was a life totally different from the world she was used to.

"How often do you..." She broke off, giving me one of her adorably shy smiles. "I mean, how often do you, uh, *transform?*"

I laughed. "It's good to shift at least a couple of times a month, otherwise my wolf gets a bit antsy, but most of the time it just happens, y'know? Running on two legs can get boring."

She chuckled. "Fair enough."

"It's different for everyone, I guess. Apparently Allara wasn't in wolf form for *years*, and she *still* got close to beating Reid's ass," I snickered. "According to my sister, anyway."

"Can I meet her?" Tammy said. "Her name's Kara, right?"

My stomach flipped. I must have looked unsure or something, because Tammy's expression dropped in an instant.

"Oh, God, I'm so sorry. That was forward of me."

"No!" I cut in quickly. "No, you'll meet her later, I promise. I don't know where she is right now, is all. She's gone off somewhere, probably with..."

Naomi.

Jesus, this was gonna get complicated if I didn't play my cards right.

Naomi arriving here a split second after Tammy showed up and I bonded with her, was like some kind of cosmic bad joke.

"Never mind," I finished lamely. "We can hang out today, though."

I had to stop myself from saying *if you want,* like some kind of awkward teenager. I couldn't help it. Tammy made me feel clumsy, like I was putting the moves on someone for the very first time, and doing it very poorly.

"I'd like that," Tammy said softly. My hand found hers where it rested against the couch cushions, and I laced our fingers together, squeezing tightly. "Very much," she said, and the warmth in her tone chased my awkwardness away.

TAMMY

Jason's plaid shirt was a little long in the arms, but other than that it fit me okay. The material was soft, and I couldn't stop running my hands over it as we talked.

It was distracting, wearing his clothes. The scent of him all around me was heaven.

It made my heart race when I saw his eyes lingering over my frame, drinking in the sight of me. It made me feel special. Wanted.

In spite of that, I hadn't been able to bring myself to get changed in front of him this morning.

You're being ridiculous. You've slept together, what do you have to hide?

But it had been very dark in the forest the night before. And I wasn't sure I was ready for him to see *all* of me in the cold light of day.

As much he seemed to want me, I couldn't fully trust in this Fated Mates bond thing, quite yet. I sighed to myself. My insecurities over my body had always gotten in the way of me feeling comfort-able in my previous relationship. Sex with my ex *always* happened with the lights off, no exception, and he had always made it clear he wanted me to lose more than a few pounds.

Jason's gorgeous body didn't exactly help matters. He would never understand the insecurity that came with not being overly attractive, and I wouldn't expect him to.

Things were so warm and safe between us this morning. He was so beautiful, his expression open and happy as we talked.

I didn't want to screw things up, but the worst part of it was, I *knew* that I would.

I always did. It was inevitable. Now and always.

Only this time, when things ended with Jason, I had the feeling it would hurt a whole lot more than anything I'd ever experienced. There was good *and* bad about being someone's Fated Mate.

"You're doing that thing again." He reached out and pushed a lock of hair behind my ear. My skin tingled at his touch, the sensa-tion lingering long after he withdrew his hand. "What are you thinking?"

"What thing?" I deflected, tucking my feet up under me.

"Like at the bonding ceremony," he explained. "You looked... I don't know. Sad. Regretful."

Inwardly I flinched at his perception, but I made sure my facial expression didn't show my discomfort. "I told you, I was happy for my friend."

He was silent, waiting for me to say more.

"Doesn't everyone have some sort of damage, Jason?" I said eventually, and let out a deep sigh. "It's... complicated."

He frowned. I could see his concern for me was growing. His brow furrowed as if he was trying to figure me out and not quite succeeding. "Try me."

I bit my lip, hesitant. "It's a long story."

He slid his arm along the back of the couch and brushed his fingers against the nape of my neck. The evocative touch made me melt into him even further, and he shot me a crooked grin, clearly pleased at the reaction he'd elicited.

"I've got time," he said simply.

"Okay." I paused, giving myself a moment to gather my thoughts. "Well, I guess I should start at the beginning. I was sixteen when I started dating Johnny." I stared into the distance as the memories flooded my head. "We were high school sweethearts."

I caught Jason's eye, and he nodded. He was listening with that unique, wolf-shifter intensity of his, giving me his undivided attention.

"No one thought it would last, but we dated all through high school, then college." I sniffed. "I believed that I'd found the man I would marry. We talked about it plenty... where we'd have the wedding, what kind of cake we'd have, all that stuff." I let out a laugh, cringing a little at the broken sound. "It seems so stupid now, saying it out loud. Then, on the night before my college graduation, I came home to find him in bed with another woman."

My eyes flicked up to ascertain Jason's reaction to my words. His face was impassive, but there was an angry steel in his eyes that made me shiver. I glanced away again.

"Cliché, right?" I shrugged, trying to hide my hurt. "Turns out he'd been seeing Christine—a woman from his office—behind my back for over six months," I said grimly. "The worst part of it was the way he yelled at me after I walked in on them. Like it was somehow *my* fault I'd caught him screwing around with someone else. In our bed."

"What an asshole," Jason growled, and I huffed out a fake chuckle.

"He said he was going to tell me after I graduated. Apparently, he didn't want to *distract* me from my studies." I couldn't keep the bitterness out of my voice. "After that, he told me we were over. That he was leaving me."

"Good riddance." Jason's eyes were hard, burning with their usual intensity. "At least the trash took itself out."

My chest warmed at his protectiveness, which cut through some of the resentful residue left by Johnny's betrayal. I shook my head, fiddling with the hem of my shirt. "I guess. It didn't feel like that at the time, though." *Still doesn't.*

"So... Reid and Allara's perfect relationship, and their bonding ceremony..." He trailed off, waiting for me to fill in the blanks.

"Yeah, it kinda stung a little, even though I was so happy for them both." I looked him in the eye, proud of the way my voice held steady. "All my dreams for the future, the life I'd built with the man I thought I was going spend the rest of my life with, disappeared, just like that."

Jason nodded, seeming to understand. His index finger traced random patterns across the back of my hand. I focused on the comfort of his touch, letting it soothe me before I went on.

"Meanwhile, Allara's childhood sweetheart comes out of nowhere to sweep her off her feet. They have a beautiful ceremony, they're perfect for each other in every way..."

"I can see how that would be hard to watch," Jason murmured. "It's *normal* to feel the way you felt, after what happened to you."

"And yet, I still felt like an asshole," I said flippantly, giving him a rueful smile. "Allara found the one person she was destined to be with, right in front of her. Imagine being that lucky."

"Ah, hello? Fated Mate over here." He waggled his hands and raised his brows, and all of a sudden my heart lightened.

I giggled, then sobered. "It's not quite the same thing, you and I, is it?" Allara and Reid were from the same world, an Alpha and a Beta, destined to be together in every way.

Jason and I were worlds apart—literally. And I knew, deep down, that this thing between us could only ever be temporary.

"Well... sometimes things don't shake out in exactly the way you think they will," Jason pointed out. There was a twinkle in his eye when he spoke. "Doesn't mean you should close yourself off from the world forever."

"Are we still talking about *me* right now?" I tilted my head, watching his expression change to puzzlement, then defensiveness.

"What do you mean?"

"Maybe you're right," I said. "I got burned by a guy, and it's been haunting me ever since. But you're haunted too, Jason." I leaned forward. "I can see it. There's a sadness in you, too. What happened with Jaime?"

He ducked his head, his hair falling over his face. I brushed it away, tilting his chin up so I could look into his eyes.

"You can't change the past," I said. "Neither of us can. We have to carry on."

He surged forward and captured my lips. I wrapped my arms around his neck, holding him close. There was a desperation inside me as I kissed him and I could feel equal desperation in Jason. I wondered if I would ever get tired of this. The thrill of having a guy so attractive want me as much as I wanted him.

I was giddy with it. I would take whatever he gave, for as long as he gave it.

There's more to it than that, isn't there? A small voice said, coming from somewhere in the back of my mind.

You just don't want to admit it to yourself, but it's true. You're falling for him. Hard. Even though you've only really just met.

CHAPTER 14
TAMMY

The next week with the pack flashed by in a blur. Allara had sent someone to the city to collect some of my things, so I now had some more of my own clothes and personal belongings, which was easier than borrowing stuff from others.

I managed a couple of static-filled phone conversations with Mick and Penny from Rachel's ancient landline, just to let them know I was doing okay. From her tone of voice, I quickly realized that Penny *knew* that Allara was a wolf shifter, and that she was the Alpha of the pack.

I rolled my eyes when she said, "Oh my God, I am sooo jealous right now! I can't believe you're sleeping with one of them! How hot is that?"

She should try being in my shoes for a minute.

I couldn't deny that being with Jason was going great—way easier than I expected, actually—but I couldn't stop the niggling doubts. When would the penny drop for him, that I didn't belong here?

I lay awake late at night, soaking in the warmth of Jason's arms around me. It was a struggle to believe that it could always be like this. The two of us, here, a human and a wolf shifter. Side by side. Forever.

It was hard enough to make a relationship work when you were both the same. But other than the couple of phone calls, I was completely cut off from the outside world. And the weird thing was, I didn't mind one bit.

Nobody objected to me taking over the schoolhouse and giving lessons to the kids. A few days in, I realized that wolf shifter kids *really* didn't like being confined to a classroom all day.

After that, I tried to keep their curriculum as outdoorsy as possible, collecting jars of tadpoles and sketching different types of leaves while we sat out in the fresh air, letting them run around and burn off some of that endless energy in between lessons.

Some of the adults continued to give me suspicious glances every so often, but those grew fewer and fewer as the days wore on, especially when the children seemed to enjoy their lessons and kept coming back each day for more. To be honest, the pack adults seemed relieved to have the kids occupied rather than getting underfoot or running amok like wild things. The fact that I was a human, was apparently something they were willing to overlook.

There was one woman, however, who never seemed to want me around.

She was Kara's best friend, back for a visit. Naomi.

She was tall, slender, and toned, like all the shifter women, with long, wavy hair the color of honey. She never spoke to me, but I saw the way her eyes flashed whenever I walked into a room. The perfect shape of her mouth twisted, like she'd caught the scent of something she didn't like.

I tried not to let it bother me, but it was difficult. She was way too obvious about her dislike of me. And ignoring beautiful women was not easy for me. It took a level of confidence I didn't have.

There was something else about the woman that bothered me. I didn't like the way she talked to Jason, one hand resting loose against his elbow, leaning into him.

She was familiar with him, clearly. *Intimately* familiar. And she was at pains to make sure I knew it.

Every time they were together, it was like she was marking her territory. Telling me without words that there was something between them. I was powerless, watching her hands move over his arms with casual confidence.

The worst part was, I *couldn't* match her actions.

I didn't know how to touch him like that. I wasn't sure I had the right.

On a logical level, I knew my insecurities were skewing things between us. Jason held me so tight, night after night, worshiping my body unlike any man I'd ever known before, whispering adoration into my ears as I moaned my pleasure and we wrapped ourselves around one another.

But when Naomi was around, it brought back so many bad memories. I'd tried to forget them, but they kept bubbling up out of nowhere, disturbing my peace.

Memories of Johnny. And his other woman, Christine.

He'd loved me once, too. Or so he'd said. Until I caught him in bed, in the arms of the woman he'd sworn up and down was just a friend.

It wasn't fair to Jason, I knew that. He and Johnny were polar opposites in so many ways. Johnny had been professional and clean-cut, always in a shirt and tie. He was hard to read. Pleasant to every-one, but distant.

By contrast, Jason was as rough and ready as they came. After the soul-bonding ceremony between Allara and Reid, I hadn't seen him in anything close to formalwear. He favored plaid flannel, jeans, and solid boots, like everyone else here. He often had a five o'clock shadow, and the feel of his stubble against my skin drove me crazy with need.

He wasn't one for cologne, but he always smelled so good to me. The soap he showered with mixed in with the scent of forest foliage and a tang of something Allara told me were his shifter pheromones that were apparently perfectly aligned to my system.

You're not a wolf shifter, she explained. *But he smells so good to you because you've bonded with each other. It'll be the same for him whenever you're near.*

I'd blushed at that but decided to take the whole thing in stride. It certainly made better sense to me now why I wanted to launch myself at Naomi every time she so much as *looked* at Jason.

I wanted her greedy hands off my man.

I guess the possessive wolf thing goes both ways.

The whole thing drove me crazy, and that damn woman knew it. She was dangling him in front of me like a prize to be won, and I couldn't do a damn thing about it except watch, and seethe inside.

"WHAT'S *WITH* HER?" I asked Allara, hours later.

She looked up from where she'd been swirling her tea around in her mug, lost in thought. We were sitting on her porch, the place where I spent many evenings when Jason was out of town for work. Dusk was beginning to settle, and twilight turned the skies a pale violet above us. I could hear grasshoppers chirping in the undergrowth.

"Who?" Allara asked after a moment. She sometimes lost the thread of our conversations, too caught up thinking about pack business.

"Naomi," I whispered. "She seems to *hate* me."

"Oh," Allara snorted. "*Naomi.*"

The name in her mouth seemed to carry a lot of significance. I raised an eyebrow at her, and she sighed heavily.

"Naomi grew up across the creek. Officially, she's still part of the Thornwood pack, but she's been kind of a nomad for the past few years." When she noticed my expression, she shrugged. "Not all wolf shifters want to settle down, Tammy. Naomi... she's different."

Having lived with the pack for only a short while, I found myself struggling to imagine any other kind of life. What could be better than having a family around you, supporting you? Protecting you?

"What *aren't* you telling me?" I challenged Allara.

Her mouth twisted, but she looked amused. I think she enjoyed having me around—a human, not blood-bound by loyalty, and someone who wasn't afraid of her.

"Jason met Naomi when we were kids," Allara said. Her voice halted a little and she fiddled with the handle of her mug. "They had an on-again, off-again thing for a while. Jason might have considered bonding with her, I don't know. But Naomi..."

I waited for a minute before nudging my foot gently against hers. She shrugged.

"The point is, I don't think either of them were ever *serious* about it. Jason's never been serious before, not about anyone." She gave me a warm smile. "Before you came along, I mean."

My chest grew tight. Over the last few days, I'd felt the walls I had so carefully constructed around my heart splinter a little. Cracks were beginning to show in the protective walls, and the light was creeping in for the first time in what felt like forever.

I'd started to allow myself to believe that Jason actually *cared* about me.

It was dangerous and dizzying, but I couldn't help it. He *got* to me in a way that no one ever had before. To be honest, I was addicted.

"How can I know how he *really* feels, Allara?" I heard myself ask.

"We've only known each other for a couple of weeks. What if he gets tired and moves on?"

I hated showing this much vulnerability, but Allara was a good friend. I knew she'd understand.

"I guess you never *can* know for sure," Allara said. "But, for our kind, the soul-bond is a once in a lifetime event. It's impossible to ignore, Tammy. It means that you two are fated."

I had to admit, all the talk of *fate* and *souls* around here scrambled my head. I sighed, giving her a reluctant nod. Maybe I understood it as much as I was ever going to.

"Besides..." Allara leaned forward, shooting me a conspiratorial look. "Forget about *him* for a moment. What do *you* want, Tammy?"

"What do you mean?"

"Do you like living here with us?" Allara asked. "Does it make you happy?"

"Of course!" I wondered how anyone could *not* be happy here. "It's... it almost feels like... home."

I whispered the word, hearing the longing in my voice. Being here, I felt an overwhelming sense of peace, safety, and contentment. Some mornings I woke up and wondered how I could have gone without it for so long.

It was like I'd been walking around with a piece of me missing. And being out here, with Jason, with the pack... I felt whole.

"And your life in the city?" Allara asked. My head jerked up. "What about your grad school for social work? Have you applied yet? You told me you were working on it a while back."

"Uh..." I stalled. "I guess I haven't... quite finished it yet."

That was an obvious lie. I knew perfectly well that those forms were sitting on top of my dresser in my apartment, untouched, as they had been for months.

She raised an eyebrow at me, and I flung out my hands. "Come on, you *know* I like bar-tending! The tips are *good*—"

"They're really *not* —" Allara cut in.

"And *besides*, it's... fun." I fixed her with a determined look. Her sceptical expression didn't budge, however, and before long, my shoulders sagged with defeat. "Okay, fine. Sometimes it sucks. But..."

"You wanna know what I think?" Allara prodded me.

No... but I suspect that you're gonna tell me anyway.

"When I took that bar job," Allara said, "I was running away from something. And I think you're running too, Tammy. Maybe not from a crazy wolf pack, like I was." Allara smirked. "But you've got your own demons, I know you do. In the city, I was lost. And maybe you were, too."

I opened my mouth, ready to protest, but no words came out. I ducked my head.

"You might not be a wolf shifter, Tammy, but you fit in here. Everyone can see it." Allara rested a hand on my shoulder, ever the Alpha. I sniffed, my emotions threatening to spill over. "Maybe it's time to stop running. Things don't always work out exactly the way you think they will." She gave a snort. "*Trust* me."

"I can stay?" I whispered.

"Of course, you can!" Allara pulled me into a tight hug. After a moment, I returned it. "As long as you want."

We pulled away from each other and smiled.

Something struck Allara and she giggled.

"What?" I asked.

"You'd really be doing *us* a favor." She leveled a grin at me. "Those kids were running rings around us. We need you, Tammy. We need you as our kid wrangler."

I spluttered with laughter and shook my head, but I couldn't deny it. The idea was exciting. It meant I had a purpose here, a place. Maybe it didn't matter that I wasn't exactly like them. As Allara said, sometimes even individual wolf shifters didn't fit in with a pack. Was it really so unlikely that the reverse could be true, too?

Maybe I have, at long last, found my dream. A place to call home, for real.

~

One week turned into two, and then three.

Before I knew it, a whole month had passed. A month of waking up in Jason's bedroom. Of slow, lazy mornings, of exploring the woods and swinging around giggling children by the hands. Baking in Rachel's cozy kitchen and chatting with Allara over cups of peppermint tea.

The only dark spot in my happiness was the occasional nausea I felt creeping in here and there, disrupting my day. Herbal tea usually helped, but there were days I was about ready to throw up. Jason made me chicken one evening and it made me so queasy I had to lie down on the sofa.

A crazy thought struck me. *Could I be pregnant?*

It seemed impossible. After that first, wild time, out in the woods, we'd been so careful.

It was too much, too fast, too soon. Almost as soon as I had the thought, I pushed it to the back of my mind, unwilling to examine it any further.

I was feeling particularly rough one afternoon and I'd gone to lie on the sofa, trying to shake off the sickness that swept over me. I heard faint sounds of movement in the kitchen.

Thinking it was Kara, I called out, "Hey, Kara, would you mind bringing me a glass of water, please? I'm not feeling very well."

A voice traveled in through the open doorway. "Well, looks like you've made yourself right at home already."

The tone was pointed and full of barely concealed hostility.

I craned my neck, sitting up just enough to look over the back of the sofa. Naomi was leaning against the doorway, arms crossed, looking at me with narrowed eyes.

"Oh," I said, brushing the hair off my face. I hoped that I didn't look as much of a mess as I felt. "Sorry. I thought you were... never mind."

I heard her scoff, and I felt a twinge of irritation in my stomach.

What's her problem?

"Can I help you with something?" I sat up as straight as possible, trying to project an aura of confidence that I didn't feel.

"Not at all," she said, giving me a sweet smile that didn't reach her eyes. "You'll be gone soon enough, won't you?"

"What's that supposed to mean?" I whispered.

I felt like I had just missed a step on the stairs. I was grasping at the empty air around me, but I knew I was going to fall, no matter what.

She didn't move from the doorway, but she leaned forward, looking me right in the face. I saw the wolf in her eyes, the predator that lurked just beneath the surface.

She could tear me to shreds if she wanted to, physically and mentally.

"Jason doesn't *settle down*," she said, her voice coated with venom. "Don't make the mistake of thinking he's actually serious about you, *human*."

"You don't know anything about us," I said. I heard my voice tremble, and a slow smile spread across her face. Oh, yes. She'd heard that tremble, too.

"You're a play-thing to him," she continued, letting out a humorless laugh. "You're nothing more than a game. Think about it. Why would he settle for someone like you?"

I was silent. My mind raced and my palms began to sweat.

I shouldn't listen, but I couldn't help it. Everything she said confirmed all my worst fears. I wasn't good enough for Jason. I wasn't a wolf shifter. I wasn't slender and sexy. I didn't have stamina or agility or a killer instinct. I had none of the qualities that were prized among shifters and humans alike.

"The truth is..." She shrugged, giving me a brief, calculating glance up-and-down, before looking away, as if she couldn't bear the sight of me. "You're just a fat, unremarkable human. You don't fit in here, and you never will."

Before I could respond, she turned on her heel and sauntered out, leaving me reeling in her wake.

CHAPTER 15
JASON

The moment I stepped into the house, I could sense something was wrong.

Nothing was out of place, as far as I could tell from a cursory glance. All the furniture was exactly as I'd left it this morning. My old flannel shirt was draped neatly over the back of the sofa, and my books were stacked equally neatly on the coffee table.

Nevertheless, my eyes narrowed.

I stalked through the house and peered into every room. The kitchen, my bedroom, Kara's room... no one was home.

That was weird. Tammy was usually back by this time in the afternoon.

Maybe she got held up at the schoolhouse or something.

Still, something felt wrong in a way I couldn't put my finger on. I thought back to this morning, trying to remember if anything had felt out of the ordinary.

Nope. The past couple of days had been great.

So good, in fact, that I'd been working up the courage to ask her to move in with me permanently. I thought we could make a weekend trip to the city and pack up the rest of her things. Maybe check in on some of her friends along the way.

I wandered back into my bedroom and noticed that her handful of items, which had previously been littered over my bedside table, were gone.

My puzzlement began to give way to panic. I strode over to the window and looked out onto the assortment of trucks and dirt bikes that littered the turf outside.

My truck was still there, but...

I raced down the stairs and out the front door, snatching up the scrap of paper that was fluttering on my windshield.

Jason,

I'm sorry. I needed to get out of here. I've gone back to the city. Just give me some time to clear my head.

Please don't follow me.

Tammy

I released a growl of frustration and crumpled the note in my fist. My blood was pumping, and worry flooded through me as I pictured her out there in the woods alone.

What is she planning? To hitch a ride with some stranger?

If she'd gone on foot—and my instincts told me she had—she must be heading for the main road, which lay a couple of miles out of town. I didn't know how much of a head start she had on me, but I figured I could catch up.

My body screamed at me to shift into my wolf form. It would be faster that way. I could track her down using all my senses.

I managed with some effort to restrain myself.

She's clearly upset over something. It won't do her any good if a giant wolf comes bounding out of the forest and transforms into a man in front of her.

I leapt into my truck and turned on the ignition. Several people gave me curious glances as I trundled up the dirt road toward the highway, but no one stopped me. I caught a glimpse of myself in the rearview mirror and understood the curiosity. I looked like a madman, with my hair sticking out and my eyes glinting with silver.

Calm down!

It was impossible to calm down. Tammy was out there somewhere, alone. Before long, it would be dark. Her human senses would make it impossible for her to navigate the rough terrain.

I hurtled down the road, pressing the gas pedal hard, until the truck was flying along. The darkened trees flashed by me on either side, and I pounded the dashboard with one hand, willing the vehicle to go even faster.

I began to wonder whether I'd made a mistake. Maybe she hadn't gone on foot toward the main road. Maybe she'd persuaded Allara or Reid to give her a ride back to the city, or she'd wandered off into the woods...

But something deep in my gut told me that I was on the right path. She was somewhere along this road, I knew it.

I rounded the next corner and saw a lone figure walking by the side of the road. My brakes screeched, and the figure whipped around.

Tammy.

Her face was pale and her eyes were shadowed and red-ringed, like she'd been crying. They widened when she saw me, and her lips pressed into a thin line, like she was trying to stop herself from bursting into tears.

A strange feeling pierced through me at seeing her distress, like a blade lodging itself in between my ribs.

I exited the truck and hurried toward her, taking her face in my hands. "Tammy! *What—*"

"You followed me!" she exclaimed. To my rapidly growing bewilderment, she *glared*. "I told you not to, Jason!"

Why was she angry? What had she expected—that I'd just let her run off and not follow? Not do whatever it took to convince my mate to come back where she belonged?

I rubbed my hands up and down her arms. She was cold to the touch, only wearing the dress she'd arrived in all those weeks ago, and a thin cardigan overtop. A small bag sat at her feet where she'd dropped it when she turned.

"I was..." How could I explain the feeling of dread that caught hold of me when I read her note? Instead, I focused on the practicalities at hand. "*Why* are you out here on foot? You're freezing!"

She shrugged my hands off her. "I'm fine!"

So stubborn. "If you're not happy—" I forced my voice to sound as neutral as possible. "You should've just said something. Your note scared the daylights out of me!"

"You don't get it, Jason." To my horror, her eyes filled with tears. "I don't belong there, and I never did! And it's *stupid* to keep pretending..."

"Pretending *what?*" I felt like she was speaking a completely different language.

Where was this coming from?

"That it's going to work out between us." Her voice was trembling with suppressed emotion. "We're just kidding ourselves, Jason." Her shoulders slumped, and her voice was weak. "At the end of day, you're *you* and I'm *me*."

"What's that supposed to mean?" I asked, feeling a twinge in my stomach I felt ill, as if I were about to lose anything I'd eaten in the last day.

I thought she'd gotten over the fact that we were from two very different worlds. Clearly, she hadn't.

"It means that I'm doing us both a favor! With me gone, you'll see that..." She bit her lip as splotches of red appeared in her otherwise pale cheeks. "That there are other options. *Better* options."

I shook my head. "No. There's just you, Tammy." I took a deep breath. "It's only ever been you. The moment we met, I realized that I'd simply been waiting for you to arrive in my life."

"You think that now," she said weakly.

I wished we were having this conversation in the relative warmth of my truck. She looked exhausted and cold.

"Jason, I can't stay here."

I tried to imagine life with the pack without her in it, and I found that I couldn't. "Tammy, *please*."

"Come with *me*." Her usually soft gaze was pointed. Her brows drew together imploringly. "Let's just *go*, Jason. Back to the city, to my place. I'll never belong here, and we both know it."

I'd run out of words. All the fight fizzled out of me as I stood before this lovely, impossibly stubborn woman. I could go with her, to the city, but whatever it was holding her back from being with me, wasn't mooted in location. I had the feeling we would simply take the issue with us, even though I wasn't quite sure what the issue was.

I found myself tracing over the planes and angles of her face in my mind, committing it to memory.

"I..." She gazed up at me, and I faltered. "I don't think that's a good idea, Tammy."

Her gaze dropped. "Well, then."

"We can work this out," I said. "We *can*... just come back to the truck. At least let me get you warm."

After a moment she nodded and, in silence, we walked back to my truck. She climbed into the passenger seat with obvious reluctance. The line of her back was stiff, and her face, usually so kind and open, was shut off like the light inside her had been snuffed out.

I started the engine, letting the truck heat up inside. With Tammy, I had to constantly remind myself that she couldn't weather the harsher elements like I could. As a shifter, my body temperature ran a little hotter than a non-shifter human. Her relative fragility was kind of terrifying whenever I thought about it too much, though I was always more than happy to lend a little body heat.

"I can't leave my pack," I murmured again. "I'm sorry. It's not that I don't..." I ran a hand through my tangled hair, at a total loss. "It's my *family*."

It wasn't just Kara. If I left now with Tammy, I would be abandoning Reid and Allara at a time when they needed strong people around them. I had to prove my loyalty to them, all over again, and leaving now would send the opposite message.

"Please Tammy. I can't bear the thought of life without you in it."

She just stared at me with big, sad eyes, and I could almost hear the words in my head. *But you won't leave your pack for me.*

It was a crazy realization. I was loyal to them now. I would protect the pack until my last breath, if I had to. But in that realization, my heart was torn in two.

Tammy didn't realize what she was asking of me. She wasn't forcing me to choose between the two things that tethered me to earth, of course.

But if she left, it would likely destroy me. And if I left with her, it would likely destroy us both.

"I understand," Tammy said. Her voice was so quiet I would have missed it if I hadn't been hanging on her every word.

A small spark of hope caught in my chest. "You do?"

Does that mean she'll come back with me? Will she stay?

"Yes." She turned to me. "Could you drop me off at the nearest bus station, please?"

The spark died. Something broke inside me, a silent howl rising up in my chest, but I kept my gaze steady. I didn't want to cause her any more pain than I clearly already had.

I turned my gaze to the road and nodded, forcing out the words past the lump in my throat. "As you wish."

CHAPTER 16
TAMMY

Walking back into my city apartment after all the weeks I'd been away, I expected to feel a sense of... I don't know. Relief, maybe. Or comfort.

I was back where I belonged, after all. Back in the human world, where I knew the rules, kept my head down and never stood out as different from everyone else around me.

Closing the front door, I leaned against it and let out a heavy sigh. I dropped my bag at my feet.

After a minute, I began to open curtains and windows to allow some air through, and shook out my bedsheets. I rifled through my kitchen cupboards in search of something to eat, but aftr all this time there wasn't much left that was edible, so I gave up and ordered takeout, resolving to spend the evening watching trashy TV.

I refused, categorically, to allow the sorrow in my heart to take hold. I had done the right thing.

He deserves someone amazing. Someone strong and athletic. Someone he doesn't have to worry about every second of the day.

Someone as beautiful as him.

I ignored the gnawing ache deep inside, and picked up the university forms that still lay on top of my dresser. I took them into the living room and, with the help of the white wine that came with my takeout, I set about filling them in.

Allara is wrong.

This is my dream. It was waiting for me, right here. I got distracted for a long minute, but now I'm back where I actually belong.

I'm home.

I repeated the mantra to myself, over and over while I worked on the forms. I said it so much that, by the time I crawled into bed in the small hours of the morning, I had almost convinced myself it was true.

*J*ASON

I spent most of the following morning in a total daze.

When Kara asked me where I'd been, and where Tammy was, I dodged the question. I grabbed a piece of toast off her plate, trying to keep to normal behavior so she wouldn't ask anything more, ignored her protests and headed outside without a backward glance.

I walked around and spoke to people, like I always did. I even cracked a few jokes, I think. But I wasn't really there. I felt hollow inside, like my soul had been cut out of me and there was only an empty shell left.

All I could think about was my mate.

I'd dropped her at the bus station as she requested, and waited at a distance until the coach had pulled up and she was safely aboard before heading back to the village.

A hand landed heavily on my shoulder and I started, whirling around and automatically lowering my posture into a defensive position.

Reid put up his hands to indicate that he wasn't a threat. "Hey, c'mon man! I called your name, like, three times."

I blinked and straightened. "Sorry. I was…"

I threw out a vague hand, unable to finish. Reid seemed to catch my meaning well enough.

"Yeah, no shit," he looked me over, frowning. "You look like crap."

"Thanks," I said dryly.

The last thing I wanted to do was get into it with Reid right now. It all felt too raw, too sudden. I'd lain awake half the night and it still felt like a bad dream. Surely, I'd wake up from this soon enough?.

"Where's Tammy?" Reid asked.

My expression must have raised some alarm, because he dragged me over to the edge of the trees and looked me up and down, concern growing in his eyes.

Then he waited, eyebrows raised, and didn't say anything. Obviously, he wasn't going to let it go like Kara. I couldn't easily run from the Alpha's mate.

I drew myself up, finally ready to speak the horrible truth. "She went back to the city," I said shortly. "What can I say? I guess Fate doesn't always get it right."

The touch of bitterness in my voice masked the loneliness and loss that ate away at my insides. I wasn't used to feeling so wronged by a woman.

"Just give it some time, man," Reid said. I knew he was thinking of Allara. "She'll come around."

Reid had waited five years to get Allara back. I didn't think I'd last that long, without my mate by my side.

I wish I had the same confidence. It wasn't just the miles that separated us. A rift had opened up, and only time would tell if it could be healed.

TAMMY

I sat down heavily on the edge of the bathtub and held the small plastic wand in my hand.

I prayed under my breath to every god or goddess that I could think of, begging, *imploring* the thing to show me that my worries were unfounded.

After a minute or so, I stared blankly at the result. Two narrow lines. It was funny how such a tiny thing could make me feel like a hole had been punched through my chest.

It wasn't possible. It *wasn't...*

We'd been careful. Hadn't we?

Aside from that first time, the voice in the back of my head piped up. *You lost control, remember? He took you right there, in the middle of the woods.*

I groaned and slid to the floor, the cold bathroom tiles pressing against my butt. Getting pregnant the first time we had sex? What were the chances?

Maybe that meant we really were destined by fate? As if the constant empty sadness in my heart hadn't already convinced me of that.

I rested my head against the side of the tub and ran my fingers over those dreaded lines.

In my heart, I had already known the truth; hadn't needed to see the test result to know I was expecting. I'd known for a while, if I was being honest with myself.

I curled up right there on the bathroom floor and took stock of my situation.

I was pregnant. The father of my child was miles away, and was probably already hooked up with another woman right now. No doubt the time we spent together was just a memory to him. One chapter in a long line of his conquests. That thought made me close my eyes and press a hand over my mouth to stop the tears spilling down my cheeks.

How could I have a child here, now? How would I earn money, provide for us? My hand found my stomach and curved around it protectively as I thought about the tiny spark of life in there. It would just be the two of us.

And yet, I had never felt more alone in my life. I had no one, nothing. Every man I had dared to love had disappeared out of my life, scattered like dust in the wind.

If this was fate... then she sure had a sick sense of humor.

CHAPTER 17
JASON

There was a knock on my bedroom door and I rolled over and shoved my pillow over my head. I wanted to tell whoever it was to go away. I didn't want to speak to anyone.

After a moment, when I didn't say anything, the door creaked open.

I groaned into the pillow before removing it and rubbing my eyes, a wave of tiredness cresting through me. "Kara, I told you. Just leave me alone, will ya?"

"It's me."

My eyes snapped open and I turned my head to stare at the

intruder. I knew that voice too well.

Naomi.

I half-sat up and rested on my elbows, watching her warily as she moved through the room and sat at the edge of my bed, crossing one long leg over the other.

Her proprietary attitude annoyed me. I decided not to beat around the bush. "What do you want?"

"Wow, someone's in a bad mood." A smirk slid across her face. "You used to be so much fun, Jason. What happened?"

I didn't answer. Lying back down, I slung an arm over my face, hoping that my obvious disinterest would be enough to send her packing.

No such luck. Her voice dropped to a low, seductive purr, and my skin prickled with discomfort as she sidled closer.

"You know..." Naomi's fingers found the edge of my leg, brushing lightly against my calf atop the bedcover. "We were almost mated, once upon a time. It's not too late, Jason. I'm right here." She leaned close until I could feel her breath. "I could give you everything. I'm like you, you know that. We understand each other."

I removed my arm from over my eyes and studied her.

Naomi was perfect to look at. She had the sharp features of our kind, high cheekbones, pointed chin. Her hair was glossy and her body was lithe and toned.

I knew all this, objectively.

None of it affected me physically in the slightest.

She was pretty wrapping concealing a screwed-up present.

As gently as I could, I sat up and pushed her hand off me. I maneuvered so that we were no longer touching and leaned against my headboard.

"I'm sorry." I shook my head, rubbing a hand over my face. I just wanted her to leave so I could return to my pity party. "I just don't feel that way about you, Naomi. It might have seemed like a good idea, once upon a time. But now... no. It will never happen."

Her eyes narrowed. "Don't tell me it's because of that woman. *God,* Jason... I thought you had standards. A *human?*"

I narrowed my eyes. She didn't have the right to swan into my bedroom and talk disrespectfully about Tammy. My silence seemed to enrage Naomi.

"It was never gonna work out with her, babe." She flicked her long hair over one shoulder, fixing me with her calculating gaze. "You know that. She's not from our world. You'll be happier in the long run, believe me."

I shook my head and pointed to the door. After a long pause, she gave a huff and stood up, marching out of the room and leaving me alone in the silence.

I HOPED I could fly under the radar of the Alpha for a couple of months and do all my brooding in peace. I'd been a pariah around here for long enough, I didn't think anyone would miss me.

Unfortunately, I had no such luck.

For some reason, Lyra had gotten over her nerves around me. More than that, she'd developed an annoying habit of trailing me everywhere on the rare occasions I ventured outside my house. She kept up an endless stream of questions. Where was Tammy? When was she coming back? Did she leave because she was angry? Did I make her go away? Did she miss being around other humans? Did I know if she missed Lyra, now that she was back in the city?

I didn't have any answers for Lyra but she kept going, nonetheless.

Lyra I could deal with, and even Kara's pointed looks and attempts to get me out of the house were manageable, but Allara and Reid kept giving me searching looks, and *they* made me nervous.

Had they changed their minds about letting me stay with the pack?

Were they questioning my loyalty? Hadn't I already proven it when I watched the one woman I had ever truly *wanted,* whom I'd genuinely seen a future with, slip away?

It all came to a head one day when Allara gathered us on the steps outside the social hall to make an informal announcement.

"I'm traveling for a few days. There are some obligations I have to fulfil with a pack in Denver." Ignoring the hushed murmurs that followed her statement, she put a hand on Reid's shoulder. "In the meantime, Reid is in charge. If there are any problems, bring them to him. Got it?"

There were a few mutterings of acknowledgment and Allara nodded, satisfied. The crowd began to disperse and I turned away with them.

"Jason?" Allara called, and I swung back. Outside Kara and young Lyra, nobody had spoken to me in about a week. Everyone was giving me a wide berth, like I was an unexploded bomb that could go off at any moment. "I'll need back-up on the road. You're coming with me."

It wasn't a question. I met her solid gaze and lifted my chin, giving her a short nod.

Looks like I'm hitting the road with the best friend of the woman who broke my heart. Awesome.

I sighed. At least it would provide a distraction against the constant thoughts of Tammy. Whatever else, this trip was certainly going to be interesting.

Tammy

I spent a few listless, restless days drifting around my empty apartment in a daze.

And then, I did what I always did when life threw a curve ball my way.

I picked myself back up, dusted myself off, and made a new plan.

First off, I was keeping the baby. I knew that it wouldn't be easy, but I couldn't fathom the alternative. I'd lost Jason, I wasn't losing the only piece of him I had left.

I didn't know how it would work, of course. A wolf shifter's baby would surely be a wolf shifter. At the very least, he or she would likely have non-human traits.

I filed away all those fears, resolving to worry about them later. Jason had said shifting abilities only came about near puberty, so I had at least a decade, hopefully, before I had to figure anything out.

With a baby on the way, I wouldn't be able to continue paying the rent on this apartment.

I handed in my notice and moved in with Leah, an old friend of Mom's who lived out in the suburbs. Her kids were long since grown and her husband had died a few years back. Alone in her big house, she lived with three dogs and had a whole load of chickens in the backyard. We'd struck up an odd kind of friendship after Mom died. She had always looked out for me, especially during the low points of my life.

I was pregnant, alone, and soon to be homeless. As far as I figured, that was about as low as it got.

When she heard I was looking for a place to stay, she offered me her spare room for free. I think the arrangement suited both of us. She ended up with company and someone to cook for her, and I got a roof over my head without having to worry about how to make rent each month.

I gave up on bar work completely, instead, taking a job part-time at Penny's diner. I dipped into my savings for the rest, spending my weekends gardening in Leah's yard and sitting in my favorite armchair, staring out the window, thinking about everything and nothing.

The day I was accepted into grad school, Leah, Penny and I shared a bottle of non-alcoholic bubbly in celebration, much to Penny's disgust. We sat around the kitchen table, and I listened to the two of them talking baby names.

Try as I might, I couldn't shake the feeling that I was still... drifting.

It had been a whole month since I'd left the pack. I walked around the city streets, went to work, cooked, did laundry, and all the while felt like I was under some kind of spell.

This was the world where I belonged. A world that made sense to me. Yeah, it would be difficult, raising a child on my own. But I'd made the best of a bad situation before, and I could do it again.

My time in the forest felt like a sunlit dream. And the thing about dreams... they weren't meant to last forever. Sooner or later, I was always going to wake up.

Allara had been wrong. I wasn't Jason's soulmate and he wasn't mine. We were just two people who got tangled up with each other, taking a detour from the path we were meant to travel. But we were always destined to return to our own separate paths, in the end.

I knew all of this, for certain.

So why did it feel like an essential part of me was missing?

JASON

We'd been on the road for about an hour and my head was buzzing.

Allara sat in the passenger seat, silent. There were so many things I wanted to ask her, but I kept my mouth shut, unwilling to stoke the tension that I was afraid would overwhelm the trip if I wasn't careful.

"I know what you want to ask me," Allara said, in a calm voice.

"You do?" I shifted in my seat, uncomfortable. She was the Alpha. She probably knew everything about everyone in the pack, including me.

"You want to know if I've heard anything. From her."

I was silent. I didn't need to ask which *her* she was referring to. As usual, Allara had hit the nail on the head. I didn't want to give her the satisfaction of knowing it, though, so I let out a noncommittal grunt.

"I'm sorry, Jason," she said. Her tone was surprisingly soft. "I wish I had good news."

"I'm just trying to put it in the past," I murmured. My voice barely cut above the roar of the engine, but Allara's head jerked in acknowledgment. "Anyway, she was right. She's a human, and I'm a shifter. It was never going to work. It doesn't even make sense."

Allara didn't reply. A strange expression settled across her features. She glanced out the window, and I watched as the corner of her mouth tilted up a little.

That's kind of a weird reaction to have when someone tells you their soul-bond was doomed.

Then again, Allara *was* kind of strange.

We fell back into silence, but it was no longer an uncomfortable one. I focused on the open road for a few minutes.

"You know, I asked Reid something the other night." There was a gleam in Allara's eye that I'd only seen on rare occasions. "And his answer surprised me."

"Oh?" I couldn't keep the curiosity out of my voice.

"I asked him a simple question. If he were the Alpha, who would he pick as his Beta."

I shrugged, tapping my fingers against the steering wheel. "You, surely?"

"I wasn't in the running." Allara smiled at me, not unkindly. "It's totally hypothetical, obviously, but he told me that, if he had to pick, he would've picked *you*."

I frowned. That didn't make any sense at all.

"Why?"

Allara let out a bark of laughter, no doubt at my shocked expression. "Why *not*, Jason? You're strong, smart, and you've proven your loyalty to this pack a hundred times over." She gave me a serious look and I saw the spirit of the old Alpha—her father—reflected in her eyes. "You're a good man."

I had to blink a couple of times and I coughed once or twice. Something must've blown off the windshield into my eye. It was the only explanation as to why I felt so choked up all of a sudden.

"I didn't know you guys, uh," I flexed my hands against the wheel, unsure. "*Trusted* me so much."

I'd been on the edge of things for so long, the bad guy with a chip on his shoulder. I didn't know how to *be* anything else. Sincerity, softness... it wasn't a script I was much familiar with.

"I've seen the way you act around Tammy," Allara said. "That's all the reason I need to trust you, right there."

I noted her use of the present tense, but I didn't dare correct my Alpha. It was oddly comforting. For a moment I could kid myself that Tammy was still a part of my life.

That, when I got home, she would be waiting for me.

"I don't know what to say," I mumbled.

"I know a thing or two about divided loyalties," Allara said gently. "For what it's worth, I'm glad you stayed with us—with our pack—when all that shit went down with Jaime. And I'm glad you found Tammy."

Emotions whirling, I managed to give her a nod of acknowledgment. That seemed to satisfy her. We spent the rest of the journey in silence, but I sensed that something integral had shifted between us. Allara and Reid... and me.

In spite of how bleak everything else looked, there was a tiny glimmer of hope on the horizon at long last.

I was back in the fold. Welcomed, with open arms. I *belonged*.

I allowed a small smile to ghost across my face. *It looks like I finally have my family back.*

By the time we arrived in Denver, dusk had fallen.

It was chilly this time of year. I caught Allara rubbing her hands together, a rare acknowledgment of the temperature, as our kind didn't easily feel the cold. I turned up the collar of my jacket before following her toward the gated entrance of the large compound we'd pulled up outside.

The Denver pack resided, unusually enough for our kind, on the outskirts of the city's urban center. Like us, they had built their settlement out of materials found in the landscape around them. Scrap metal, corrugated iron and old tires formed the walls that surrounded the small community, and each house looked to be built similarly.

We followed the sound of whooping laughter to where a massive bonfire had been constructed. It towered over the pack members that gathered around it, at least six feet tall. In the fading light, it flickered and burned, stacked with crates, boxes and old furniture.

A hulking figure approached us, flanked by several others. I immediately identified the huge man in the middle as the Alpha of this pack. He and Allara exchanged a polite, if formal greeting, inclining their heads to each other and clasping their forearms in a universal show of respect.

After a few minutes, Allara moved off to talk with the Alpha alone. She signaled for me to stay put, and I did so, even if part of me was frustrated.

I should be going with her. Why did she bring me here, if not for protection?

I slouched down at the edge of the group of revelers and stared into the flames. I could feel my misery rising once more. These people were strangers to me and offered me no distraction from my state of mind.

After a moment or two I became aware of a small presence hovering near my elbow.

I looked down. A petite woman smiled up at me. She was near middle-age, with gentle, smiling eyes and a motherly expression. She was holding out a plate of cupcakes to me. I caught their aroma under the fire smoke and inhaled deeply. They smelled delicious.

"Want one?" she asked with a grin.

I nodded gratefully, suddenly aware of how starving I was. "They look good. Thanks."

I was halfway through the cake when something strange occurred to me. I stopped mid-chew, glancing down at her again.

She was watching me with a contented expression. That wasn't what stopped me in my tracks, though.

It was her eyes.

They were clear and bright, a perfectly pleasant green color. They reflected the firelight...

And that was it.

There was no unearthly tinge of silver around her pupils, no predator's glow. Nothing about her marked her as a wolf. She didn't have the sharp jawline, the arrogant tilt of the head. All the little tells that were easy to read, if you knew what to look for.

She's not a shifter.

The realization was like a shot through the chest. I felt my heart clench and then thud extra-loud, and something dangerously close to hope flooded my system.

She's human. As human as Tammy. And she seems to live here, with the pack.

"Can I help you?" she asked cheerily. She looked amused by my fairly obvious reaction, but not offended.

"Sorry, ma'am," I murmured, polishing off the rest of the cupcake and brushing the crumbs off my hands. "I'm Jason."

I extended a hand, and she took it. I wanted to apologize again for my rudeness. I was totally flabbergasted by the presence of a human right in the middle of a wolf shifter pack. In spite of recent events, I couldn't get it to make sense in my mind. It was like a hen co-habiting with a den of foxes.

"Cecily," she offered. She was assessing me with a sharp, perceptive gaze. "And what are you doing all the way out here, Jason?"

"I'm escorting my Alpha," I said. I turned to try and catch sight of

Allara in the crowd, but she was nowhere to be seen. "I can't say I'm doing a great job of it, though. I seem to have lost her."

I turned back to her with a rueful grin, and she laughed, tipping her head back. "Yes, I can see why they like you."

I'd lost the thread of the conversation somehow. This human was running rings around me, while I blundered in the dark.

They keep doing that, don't they?

I shook off that critical inner voice and refocused my attention. "Who?"

"Reid and Allara, of course." Her eyes twinkled up at me. "You have a good heart. I can tell these things."

I couldn't help but feel charmed by the lady. Other than the human thing, in many ways she really reminded me of my mom.

For many years now, it had just been Kara and me. I'd forgotten what it was like to have someone reassure me, even in such a basic way.

"Can I ask you something?" I queried. The fire in front of us flared, golden sparks flying up into the darkened skies above.

"Ask away, dear."

"You're... human." My voice trailed off, into the night air between us.

"That isn't a question." She leveled a glance at me, her expression warm. "But, yes, I am." She folded her hands and stared into the flames. "The Alpha of this pack, Embry, is my mate."

My eyebrows flew into my hairline. I didn't bother trying to hide my astonishment. An *Alpha* mated with a human? I had never heard of such a thing.

Does that mean what I think it means?

"We met by accident," Cecily explained, in her soft, lilting voice. "Bumped into each other outside a train station. At first, I thought he was crazy. He kept telling me I *had* to come with him, that it was important. I almost turned tail then and there. But..." She spread out her hands, shrugging. "There was something about him. I just couldn't get him out of my head, no matter how hard I tried."

"You're bonded to him?"

She nodded. "Our children are shifters, like him. I like to think they got some of their better traits from me, though." She twinkled at me again. "When they've got themselves filthy from playing outside, they're *his* kids."

A booming voice sounded from somewhere behind us. "She's right. Their better traits are definitely from their mom."

I jumped to my feet, turning as I did. Embry, the Alpha, pressed a kiss to the top of his mate's head and gave me a short nod. I touched my hand to my chest in a sign of deference.

"Embry, meet Jason." Cecily stood up, sliding her small arm around his waist. Even standing, she didn't quite reach his shoulder. "I was telling him about the day you and I met."

The Alpha's face turned soft and fond, a surprising expression on such a big, stoic man. "I guess it was a little unusual."

"It's clearly worked out for you, though," I pointed out. They both chuckled.

"It has had its ups and downs." Cecily tilted her head, resting it against Embry's upper arm. "But so does every relationship. He's a shifter, I'm a human... but we're right for each other. And at the end of the day, *that's* what matters. All the other stuff? It's just window dressing."

I couldn't argue with that, especially when I saw the expression in Embry's eyes as he stared down at Cecily. I had rarely seen two people more clearly in love with each other than these two.

Allara wandered over, a drink in her hand. When I made eye contact with her, the corners of her mouth lifted in what looked like a satisfied smirk.

Something hit me out of nowhere. It was totally obvious in hindsight. I couldn't believe that it had taken me so long to see it.

This is a set-up!

Allara had brought me here for one reason, to meet Embry and Cecily. She didn't need my protection. She'd wanted me to see that the situation I was in, that seemed so impossible to reconcile, could work out just fine, if only I would let it.

It was possible for a human to live in the middle of a wolf pack.

Not just live, but *thrive*. Have children, raise them in safety, and become a valued and loved member of the community in her own right.

I couldn't believe Allara had tricked me like this. She'd used my loyalty to her advantage, and I'd walked right into it.

Still, I couldn't bring myself to be mad at her. She had obviously done it with Tammy's and my best interests at heart. And I knew as well as she did, that if she'd been upfront with me, I would never have come. I'd been shut up in my house for weeks now, wallowing in my own self-pity.

Hope began to stir somewhere inside. Seeing Cecily and Embry's successful relationship firsthand changed things. If they could do it...

Why not Tammy and me?

Even *thinking* her name struck a chord of loss somewhere deep inside me. I knew I had to see her again, touch her. Make her mine in every way possible. Prove to her that she was the one I wanted, now and forever, and that I could make her happy, if she'd let me.

I didn't care that she was a human. It had never bothered me, except insofar as it had made her feel like she didn't belong.

All those worries at the start about her not fitting in, not finding her place with us, had turned out to be totally *wrong*. She did belong with us and, looking back, I knew she had been happy living in the village.

Why did I let her go so easily? Why had I not tried to convince her to stay?

It was me who had been too much of a coward to let her in fully, to let her know, truly, how I felt about her.

There had to be a chance that she still felt something for me.

I wasn't done fighting. For her. For *us*.

For the life we could have together.

And if she wanted to stay in the city, then I would stay there, too. *She* was my destiny; my future. I didn't care where we ended up; I just knew I needed her by my side again.

I felt a fire kindling inside me. It wasn't over. Not yet.

I knew exactly what I had to do.

CHAPTER 18
TAMMY

The day had started like every other.

Just another morning, adding to the countless mornings I had woken up since I'd left Jason. Ordinary hours passing by in my ordinary life.

As usual, I got up, ate breakfast, and got dressed in my new tailored jacket and trousers. I waved goodbye to Leah and headed out the door before eight. I liked to arrive a little early to give myself a chance to prepare for the rigors of the day ahead.

I'd been accepted into my post-graduate course and was working part time around my studies, at the local social worker's office. Just answering the phones and making appointments, but I loved the people. And it was great experience for when I graduated.

I was right where I wanted to be.

So why do I feel like a zombie?

Images of the future crept into my brain without warning. I could see the next five to ten years mapped out in front of me with startling clarity.

My baby would arrive in the late summer. I pictured the makeshift nursery, the sleepless nights. Finding a kindergarten, reading school reports, swimming lessons, pushing a tiny bike down a long drive. Watching him or her blow out a cake with two candles on it, then three, then four.

As I drove to work, I pictured breaking the news to Jason.

I couldn't even imagine it. That small town in the woods felt so far away, almost like it didn't exist at all.

The pain of those memories flared up, sharp and hot, but I suppressed them as best I could.

My child wouldn't grow up with a father who had one foot permanently out the door. That much, at least, I could guarantee. My baby would be surrounded by adults who provided unconditional love and support. People whose loyalties weren't divided between their pack and their loved ones.

I wasn't going to compromise any more. I wanted someone who would fight for me. Love *me* as fiercely as I loved the child growing inside me. And I wouldn't settle for anything less.

I would choose my own path from now on, and count my friends among those who were there for me when I needed them most.

I pulled up in the parking lot of the office building where my reception job was based. I could see the first clients through the window already. A family of two, mother and daughter.

I got out of the car and walked inside.

"Hey, Julie!" I smiled at the tiny girl with pigtails and she lit up when she saw me, bouncing up and down in her plastic seat. "How are you today?"

Julie's mom, Rosa, put an arm around her daughter and squeezed her shoulders. "She's a bundle of energy, I'm sorry." She threw me a chagrined smile.

"Oh, please don't apologize," I shook my head fervently. "I love it! I wish I were that much of a morning person."

I wasn't lying. I *did* love my work, and seeing children like Julie.

But it wasn't the life-defining passion I had once thought it would be. It was... perfectly fine.

And that's good, right? That's more than most people get. You should be grateful.

I turned away from them, toward the check-in desk. I fished my lanyard out of my bag and slid it around my neck, then almost slammed right into the guy waiting up ahead of me.

I put my hands out, prepared to launch into a volley of apologies. "I'm *so* sorry, I didn't see..."

My words died in my throat when the man turned and I got a good look at him.

It was Jason.

His hair and beard had grown out a little in the weeks we had been apart, and he looked weather-beaten, like he'd been spending even more time outside than usual. But other than that, he was just as I remembered. Well-worn jeans, sturdy boots, and a plaid shirt. A world away from the office environment we stood in. I ran a hand over the edge of my neatly pressed blouse, suddenly self-conscious.

The other receptionist, Stacy, poked her head out from behind him and caught my eye. "Tammy, do you know this guy? He came in a couple minutes ago, saying you guys know each other." She glanced at him and then mouthed, "Do you want me to call security?"

"It's fine, Stacy." I took a deep breath. My eyes returned to Jason's piercing gaze. Those eyes—both hazel and silver versions—had haunted my dreams. Right now, they were like a dagger through the heart. "He's..."

I paused, unsure of how to finish. *A friend? Ex-boyfriend? My soulmate?*

"I know him," I said eventually. "It's okay."

Hearing the weight in my words, Stacy tilted her head to the side then she shrugged. "You're in early, anyway. Take your time."

Maybe I could use the staff room to chat with him for a minute.

My brain scrambled through possible explanations for what he was doing here; what he could want.

Answers? Gas money? A map? He was here in the middle of the city. Maybe he was lost.

He probably wants his shirt back. You know, the one you keep under your pillow at night.

I fought down the blush that threatened to rise in my cheeks and tried to get a handle on the situation. The sheer fact of his presence here was enough to send me reeling.

This was my world. The human world.

He looked as out of place here as I was deep in the forest among the wolf pack.

You didn't feel out of place there, a traitorous voice reminded me. *You felt like you'd come home.*

Despite his obvious discomfort, he looked me straight in the eye. There was nothing overconfident in his demeanor. The snarky guy I had first met back at the bonding ceremony had vanished. He looked calm, steady. In spite of the circumstances, there was an openness in his expression I hadn't seen before.

"Stacy, is it okay if I use the staff room to chat with Jason for a minute?"

The other receptionist nodded, indicating to the files in front of her. "Yeah, of course. I've got this."

"This way," I said, pointing down the corridor that led to the staff room. I didn't bother asking him anything. Out here, it felt too public. There were too many curious eyes and ears.

Silently, he followed me. He kept a respectful distance between us, but I still fancied I could feel his warmth radiating against my back the whole way down the hall.

I opened the door and told him to take a seat on the sofa next to the fridge. I internally debated taking a seat behind at the table. It felt too formal, too defensive. In the end, I perched awkwardly on the edge of the dining table, pushing aside some files as I did so.

"You've cut your hair," Jason said.

His voice was decidedly neutral. I couldn't get a read on his intentions at all.

Does he like it? Is he happy to see me? Sad? Bored?

I decided to ask the obvious question. "What are you doing here?"

He looked down at his hands, turning them over, like he was trying to find the answers in his palms. I ached, wanting nothing more than to slide off the desk and take those big hands in mine and hold them close, feel his fingers cradle my face like they had done so easily, so instinctively, not so long ago.

Finally, he looked up. "I needed to see you."

I fought back the emotions that welled up inside me. Even his mere presence was enough to quiet the panicked voice buried deep inside my chest, that emptiness that had me lying awake at night, wondering if he was okay.

"Tammy," he spoke again, and my attention returned to the present moment. "I wanted to give you space. I tried to stay away from you. I thought if we went back to our separate lives, maybe this feeling would fade over time." He drew a deep breath. "I'm not strong enough to stay away from you anymore."

I froze.

Whatever I had been expecting to come out of his mouth, it wasn't *that.*

"What are you saying?" I whispered.

He leaned forward on the couch, forcing me to meet his gaze. Even though I was the one in the dominant position, I felt cornered. I crossed one leg over the other, trying to exude a control over the situation that I didn't feel.

"I'm saying that being apart from you isn't an option for me." His voice rumbled out of his chest and I shivered. "I can't do it. So, either you're gonna have to force me out of here right now, or we work this thing out."

I gaped at him. All my careful plans for the coming years were crumbling before my eyes. I hadn't factored Jason into the equation.

Then again, Jason had never failed to surprise me in the past.

It's one of the things I love about him.

I turned the thought over in my head and realized that it was true. Terrifying, *impossible*, but true. I loved him, completely and utterly.

In some ways, I still barely knew him, but it didn't matter. I *loved* him.

Unbidden, my hand slid over my belly. Jason's eyes tracked the movement without comprehension.

"What did you have in mind?" I asked in a small voice. "My work... my *life*... it's here, Jason. I'm *happy*."

His eyebrows drew together and his head fell forward, his curls tumbling. It was such a familiar sight. One that I'd missed so much.

"Okay," he said. "Then I'll come to you, Tammy. I'll pack up and move to the city for you. I don't care where I live, I just want us to be together."

I thought about the wolf shifters. Each pack was different, but I remembered Allara telling me that forest dwellers particularly struggled in urban centers. The noise, all the bright lights... it drove their elevated senses haywire.

"You would do that?" I asked. "For me?"

I was struggling to raise my voice any louder than a whisper. I worried that if I spoke at full volume, I would break the spell and this fragile thing between us would snap like a matchstick.

"Anything, Tammy." Jason reached out and put his hands over mine. When I didn't resist, he tugged one of them toward him, tangling our fingers together. Warmth flooded through me, and the emptiness I'd carried for so long dissipated. "I'd do anything, go anywhere. I don't care, as long as I'm with you."

I thought of all the careful plans I'd made, the life I'd laid out for myself in his absence.

I pictured the forest, which stretched out in my mind's eye. Mysterious, endless, full of promise and adventure.

Home.

"What about the pack?" I asked. Part of me still wanted to test him. We had been away from each other so long. Whatever he felt for me, I knew his loyalties would always lie with them.

His expression shadowed. "It will be... difficult," he conceded. "I want you to come back with me, Tammy. But I know that's not what you want."

I swallowed, watching him rise from the couch completely and erase the space between us. His hands slid either side of me, resting on the table. I looked up at him, his proximity making me dizzy.

"I..." I trailed off. "I don't know what to say."

"I know you didn't ask for this." He flung out a hand, indicating between us. "Me coming into your life, our bond. Any of it. But I can't keep pretending any more. I'm done. I can't hide the way I feel."

I leaned into his heat, unbidden. It had been only about six weeks, but it felt like forever. He was intoxicating. Suddenly, I couldn't fight against it any longer. I was tired of pretending I didn't care. "Then don't," I whispered. "I'm right here, Jason."

His hands came up to brush the hair out of my face. One of his thumbs traced down the soft part of my jawline, ghosting around the outer corners of my mouth.

"Tammy." His gaze was serious, his eyes scorching. "I love you."

His mouth met mine, searching at first. It wasn't enough. My fingers grasped the collar of his shirt and dragged him closer, and the kiss rapidly deepened into something heated and desperate.

I broke away with a gasp, leaning my forehead against his. "I love you too." I giggled, light-headed and giddy. I was floating. "I'll... I'll come back, Jason. You don't have to choose."

Jason *loved* me.

He loved me so much he was willing to give up everything he'd ever known in order for us to be together. To leap into the unknown, to build a new life for himself. For *us*.

Suddenly, every reason I had for leaving the pack seemed tiny and insignificant. All of Naomi's words, so spiteful and vicious in my memory, faded away. They couldn't hurt me anymore. They didn't matter.

Because, to Jason, I wasn't some low-grade amusement. I wasn't a fling that he had bedded and abandoned when he grew bored of me.

As it turned out, he couldn't live life without me. And I felt exactly the same way.

"You'll come back?" he asked. His voice was full of wonder. His arms drew around me, pulling me up off the desk and into a tight hug. He lifted me up off my feet a little, and I squealed. "You'll come home?"

"Yes!" I kissed him again, reveling in the luxury of it. I *could* kiss him again, touch him. I could do anything.

We could do anything.

"What about all this?" His eyes flickered around my office, taking it all in. "I thought this was your dream."

"I thought so too," I shrugged. "But the truth is, I think I've been pretending. I've been pretending that all my plans would work out exactly the way I expected them to. Pretending that I would be better off without you in my life." I drew him closer. We stood there, holding each other, for a long moment.

"I'm not okay without you," I admitted huskily.

Jason paused, and then let out a chuckle. "I guess I didn't see you coming. You took me by surprise."

"You threw a monkey wrench into my plans, too." I smiled. "Guess you can't argue with destiny."

He drew back just enough to look me in the eye. His gaze had turned serious again, roaming over every inch of my face. "It's not because of fate, or prophecy. I'm *choosing* you, Tammy. I'm choosing you for *you*."

In all my life I'd never heard anyone say those words to me. I could feel myself let go, surrender to the reality of loving him, and for once it didn't terrify me.

It was time to trust him now, with everything.

IT WAS SURPRISINGLY short work to pack up the life I'd built for myself over the past six weeks in the city.

Jason and I ended up staying for the week with Leah. I had to tie up loose ends with work; and organize to defer my studies for a year.

The other stuff—the people I would be leaving behind—that was much harder.

I said my goodbyes to Leah and Penny, who both hugged me tightly and made me promise to keep in touch. From the way they behaved, you would think I was disappearing into the forest, never to be seen again. I assured them I wouldn't be a stranger, struggling to make my point while balancing the stack of boxes I carried in my arms.

Penny placed my favorite cherry pie on top of the pile, which made the whole thing severely unstable. Luckily, Jason swooped in before I dropped the load and took everything out of my hands. He paid particular interest to the pie on his way to the truck, and out of the corner of my eye I caught Penny batting his hands away from it before he could dig into the thing himself.

The sight made me chuckle. I had a healthy appetite myself, but the wolf shifters were on a *whole* other level.

Leah drew me aside in the midst of the chaos. Her kind eyes betrayed a quiet concern. I knew she was happy for me, but I couldn't help but feel bereft, leaving her like this.

She had taken me in when I had nothing, no one. I pulled her into a hug and murmured my thanks against her shoulder. She stroked my hair, just the way I remembered Mom used to.

"Are you going to tell him?" she whispered, quietly enough so that only the two of us could hear.

I nodded. *Yes.*

I had to, and sooner rather than later. It wouldn't be long now before the physical evidence would be impossible to hide.

Leah caught my eye, and I could sense that she wanted to say more. Advice, maybe. Or a word of warning for the dangerous new world I was about to enter?

Before she could, however, Penny launched herself at me. I giggled, catching her before she could bowl us both over.

"I'm coming to visit you guys." She grinned toothily. "As soon as —" Cutting herself off, she glanced around. Jason was busy strapping my luggage down on the roof of the truck, none the wiser. "*You know what,*" she finished in a stage whisper, pointing at my stomach.

"Sooner, I hope." My smile for Penny was broad and genuine. She had become a good friend to me, and I would miss her.

"Don't keep *all of them* to yourself." Penny reached out and squeezed the bicep of an alarmed-looking Jason before bursting into laughter. "You and Allara better not forget about me, that's all I'm saying."

I shook my head, unable to stop myself giggling. Her laughter was infectious. "We could never forget about you, Penny."

After that, there was nothing more to do. No more goodbyes to be said, no more suitcases to be packed. We were waved off from the sidewalk, and in the rearview mirror I watched my friends grow smaller and smaller before they vanished from view completely.

"You okay?" Jason glanced over at me. One of his hands left the steering wheel, coming to rest in the space between us, palm upwards.

I slid my hand into his and squeezed it in response. "Yeah. I'm more than okay."

I was finally, truly, happy.

CHAPTER 19

JASON

After spending a week in the city, my offer to move there permanently began to seem more and more crazy.

A week was more than enough. The noise of the traffic, the bright neon signs, the humans and all their chaos...

I didn't know how Allara had coped for so long.

I couldn't help but be relieved that Tammy was returning to the pack with me after all. The fact that she actually seemed *excited* about it made me happier than I had any right to be.

We said goodbye to her human friends and hit the road, settling into a companionable silence that I had missed. It was the simple things that made me feel so good. My hand in hers, the open road ahead of us, and her presence by my side.

Sure, we may have problems along the way, but Cecily's voice rang in my ears. *It's all just window dressing.*

As we left the city behind us, Tammy turned to me. The expression on her face was radiant, but there was a touch of nervousness in her eyes. She looked like she was hanging onto the edge of something and she was suddenly unsure of how to let go.

"What's the matter?" I murmured, bringing her hand up and pressing a kiss against her skin.

The sunset glowed ahead of us, lighting up the landscape with golden rays. The forest looked beautiful, like it had caught fire.

"Nothing," she said. "Um, can you pull over for a minute? I have something to tell you."

My heart stuttered. She hadn't changed her mind, had she? My heart couldn't bear it. Quickly, I pulled in to the verge and turned to her. "Tell me."

She smiled at me with those gorgeous, shining eyes. "It's all good. At least, I think it is." Her smile turned shy. "I'm pregnant, Jason. We're going to have a baby."

A wave of shock hit me, followed by a pure wave of elation that made me grip the steering wheel tightly. Thank God she got me to pull over. I might have crashed the truck, otherwise. "That's... that's..."

I couldn't speak, but I shot her a huge grin, hoping it conveyed my joy.

"I know, Jason." Her hand came up, gently curving against my cheek. I focused on the gentleness of her touch, letting it soothe the pounding of my heart. "I love you."

"I love you more," I murmured. I wanted to kiss her properly. Tangle my fingers in her beautiful auburn hair and make her swoon, but this spot on the side of the highway wasn't the best place to express how I felt. I settled for turning my head and kissing her palm. "That is the best news I have ever heard, Tammy."

"You're happy?" she asked, her eyebrows flickering up as though she was still a little unsure.

I laughed. "I wish I could show you just how happy... but I think that will have to wait until I get you home and into our bed."

Tammy laughed happily and settled back into her seat, one hand spread over her still flat stomach.

I covered her hand with mine and left it there for several seconds, imagining what our child might look like when it arrived. Boy, or girl? I didn't care. I just knew I would love it as much as I loved Tammy.

I finally tore my gaze away from my beautiful mate and started the car once again. We had a long journey ahead of us, after all.

Tammy. Me. The baby. But we would make it. Together.

We were going home.

Read on for a sneak peek of:

Destiny of the Wolf

Book 3 in the 'Pack Loyalty' series

CHAPTER 1
KARA

I was on edge today. Not for any reason I could put my finger on. The atmosphere around me, inside me, just felt tense, like the air before a storm.

Across from me, on the other side of the lawn, Allara sat with her feet up, watching over the children running about. Although her body language was lazy, I could tell that she was on alert in the way that Alphas always were, scanning for threats over at the tree line.

Not that she could spring into action right now, though. Not in her condition. The sundress she wore couldn't hide her large, round belly. She chewed her bottom lip, deep in thought over something.

Reid, her mate, crossed the lawn to join her, carrying two large glasses of lemonade. Allara accepted one, smiling up at him with a softness she reserved only for him. He bent his head to press a kiss to her lips. His fingers were gentle as they slid through her hair. Surprising for such a big man.

Bitterness spiked through my chest and it only took me a second to realise what it was.

Envy.

As Reid and Allara got to talking, I bent my head over my needle-work and tried to shake the feeling away.

Those two had always known that they were fated to be together. Ever since we were kids.

Unlike them though, I'd never had even an inkling of that feeling towards anyone in the pack. I'd never experienced the pull they all talked about. That unshakable certainty that *this* shifter was the one for me.

So, I kept to myself. The other members of the pack didn't bother with me, which suited me just fine. It ran both ways; most of the time, I was happy enough in my own company.

Since my brother Jason had found Tammy, I'd withdrawn even more. It wasn't anyone's fault I didn't feel right in company anymore. Besides, it meant I had more time to work on my art.

I smoothed a hand over the pattern I was working on: dozens of trees embroidered in shades of green. The forest scene would eventually become part of a quilt for Allara's baby. The room they had planned for him or her, was spectacular.

Yeah. I have all I need, right here.

Allara and Reid were still deep in conversation. Even from this distance, I could see they were arguing about something. Allara's brow creased. It was an expression I knew well.

She doesn't want to hear whatever he's saying, but she knows he's right.

Sure enough, a few moments later, Allara threw up her hands.

Fine, fine.

Reid sat back, satisfied, and I smothered a laugh. Allara wasn't one to lose a fight and she wouldn't take it well. Reid brushed his hand against hers, and she relented, tangling their fingers together. Like all their disagreements, it was over before it had really started.

I shook my head and returned to my embroidery.

Kids on the lawn played under the watchful eye of half a dozen shifters. Beyond the grass, a group of pack members emerged from the trees carrying a deer between them.

At the other end of the village, the vegetable garden was blooming; come autumn, we would be laden with fresh fruit and vegetables.

Everything was exactly as it should be.

So why did I feel so unsettled?

Is it my imagination, or can I smell a storm on the horizon?

It WAS late evening by the time Allara and I were alone and we could catch up properly. We sat on her porch together drinking iced tea and listening to the cicadas flitting in and out of the grass around the house.

Allara had one hand on her belly, and the other absently stirred her drink.

"It's any day now, Kara." She patted her stomach and grinned. "Ugh, I'm so *done* being pregnant."

I chuckled as I remembered how Tammy had gotten in the weeks leading up to her due date. Jason had almost been as bad. Setting foot in that house was like waiting for a bomb to go off towards the end. By the time baby Mae had finally arrived, we were all at our wits' end, only to be greeted with the most placid, easy-going kid ever.

I took a sip of tea. "How's Reid holding up?"

Allara shrugged. A smile played about the corners of her mouth. "Put it this way, I'm gonna miss having him wait on me hand and foot. Though it has started to get a little ridiculous—he carried me into the *bath* yesterday. Like, actually ran me a bath and *put* me in it."

We both laughed aloud this time. How well Reid treated his mate came as no surprise to me. Few men looked at a woman the way Reid looked at Allara.

Her smile slowly faded, and her eyebrows pinched together. "Honestly, I'm frustrated. Until this baby is born, I'm stranded here. It makes my business as Alpha kind of limiting."

"Yeah." I put a comforting hand on her arm. "I can imagine."

It wasn't a situation an Alpha typically found themselves in, especially since most wolf shifter Alphas were male. As much as Allara had flourished in her role as pack leader, she now had a new priority: motherhood.

"I'm gonna confess something..." Allara turned to me, setting her drink down on a table next to her.

Her expression was serious, so I mirrored her posture.

"This isn't purely a social visit. I need to ask you a favour."

"Oh?"

Allara and I had been best friends since we were kids. We'd reconnected almost immediately after she'd returned to the pack, picking up right where we left off. The fact she was now my Alpha hadn't changed that. There was little I would refuse her.

"I've been in contact with Elder Frey, from the Thornwood Clan. He's been keeping things running round those parts, ever since..." Allara's face twisted with discomfort. "Well, you know."

Right. Their Alpha's passing.

I'd never met the Thornwood Alpha face to face, but over the years he'd nurtured an alliance with Allara's father. News of his sudden, recent death had spread like wildfire to every shifter pack in the state.

Shifter packs fiercely guarded their secrets, especially upon the death of an Alpha. But the Thornwoods had been in open disarray for months now.

"They haven't chosen a new leader yet?" I couldn't keep the

shock out of my voice. I'd never heard of such a thing—a pack running wild for so long with no sworn Alpha.

Allara's face darkened. "Oh, they had chosen one. The Thornwood Alpha's son was all set to inherit, but for some reason, on the day he was set to be sworn in, he took off."

"He... what?"

I tried to keep my face totally blank of emotion. Allara looked *pissed*, and I sensed it wasn't a good idea to point out that *she* hadn't embraced the role of Alpha with open arms at first, either.

"The truth is," Allara continued, hefting herself back in her chair with a heavy sigh, "I'm worried. Jaime's still out there, and the pack closest to our borders has no Alpha. Honestly, I don't know what he's capable of."

I caught a flicker of real fear in her expression.

I stared out at the clearing in front of us. Earlier that day, it had been full of kids playing chase, giggling and play-fighting with each other.

The thick line of trees at the edge of the grass seemed darker than usual, full of shadows. Like danger could be lurking around every branch.

I shook the thought away.

"So, what does this have to do with me?" I asked.

"Reid is going to meet with the Thornwood Clan," Allara said. "Normally, I'd go with him, but I don't feel strong enough at the moment. I want you to go in my place."

I stared at her, shocked. *"What?* Why me?"

"Because I trust you," Allara said simply. "And I need people I can trust right now. Your brother and Tammy are busy with Mae, and besides, you were my first choice."

She smiled and squeezed my hand.

"But..." I fumbled. "I don't know anything about politics!"

It was a feeble excuse, but it was true.

I wasn't like Allara—bold, confident, strong. She'd left our village without a backward glance and lived for years in a strange city. I'd always been content to spend my days here with my weaving and craftwork, making beautiful things for my community.

I couldn't just step into her role next to Reid and do the job well. There was no way.

"Kara." Allara caught my eye and held it in that instinctive, unyielding way that only an Alpha could. "Look at me. I *know* you can do this. I wouldn't have asked you otherwise."

I opened my mouth and closed it a few times.

What if I messed up? One wrong move could wreck whatever alliance Allara wanted to build and make things worse for *both* clans.

But the look on her face told me that I couldn't argue. Allara had made up her mind. More than that, I could hardly disobey a direct order from my Alpha.

"When do we leave?" I mumbled.

Allara brightened. She sat back in her chair, looking like a weight had been taken off her shoulders.

At least she's confident. That makes one of us.

"Tomorrow."

So soon? I almost squeaked. Allara caught my expression anyway and draped an arm around my shoulders, squeezing tight.

"You'll be perfect." A soft smile played around the corners of her mouth. "You'll see."

It was still dark outside when my alarm started blaring.

With a groan, I gave it a couple of smacks to turn it off. I rolled over, every muscle in my body tensed, and listened with bated breath.

There was nothing but silence from the rest of the house. I let out a long sigh of relief and allowed myself to relax into my pillows.

Tammy would never forgive me if I woke Mae up with my stupid alarm.

On the chair beneath the window, the bag I'd packed yesterday lay in wait. I glowered at it, but it didn't burst into flames. It remained exactly where it was, mocking me.

With a heavy sigh, I clambered out of bed and threw on my clothes. I was meeting Reid outside in half an hour. I had just enough time to eat some toast and brush my teeth.

There was no point waking Jason and Tammy. I'd said my good-byes to them yesterday.

Tammy had hugged me tearfully and asked when we were coming back. She didn't need to have a shifter's advanced senses to pick up on the tense atmosphere. Jason had not said anything, but his body language when he'd moved in for a hug and the way he'd squeezed me so hard my feet lifted off the floor, told me how worried he was about me going. Jason was more than a big brother to me. Since Mom and Dad had died, we were all the family we had left.

Once I had my bag on my shoulder, I glanced out the window and into the dark street. Reid was heading towards the house in the dim street lights, tension written across the broad line of his shoulders.

I knew this mission wasn't his first choice, either. He'd much rather be with Allara and his unborn child right now.

Sometimes pack duty has to come first.

I tip-toed down the stairs and shut the front door behind me as quietly as I could. Reid nodded as I came down the front steps of the house and gestured for me to follow him.

"C'mon." He hitched up his own bag on his shoulder as I fell into step beside him. "Truck's all packed and ready to go."

I stowed my bag in the bed of the truck and climbed into the passenger seat, trying not to feel awkward. It wasn't often that Reid and I were in each other's presence without Allara.

If he sensed any of my discomfort, he didn't show it. He looked a million miles away as he turned the key in the ignition and headed down the road that led out of the village. There were dark circles under his eyes like he hadn't slept in a month.

He glanced at me once we were on the main road. "All good?"

I nodded.

"We'll be back before you know it, Kara."

Judging from his expression, I could tell he wanted to believe it just as much as I did. This was the last thing either of us wanted to be doing right now. Orders were orders.

The trees rushed past as we drove. The sun began to rise, and golden light dappled the hood of the car. I tilted my head up, looking through the sunroof at the crows circling high overhead.

"What are they like?" I eventually asked, breaking the comfortable silence.

"Who?"

"The Thornwood Clan."

Reid drummed his fingers against the steering wheel. "Oh, ya know."

"No, I *don't*." I frowned out at the road ahead, avoiding his eyes. "I've never even been to the other side of the creek, Reid."

Reid's brow wrinkled. I could see he was turning my question over in his mind, trying to find the right words.

"They're...secretive. They keep to themselves, you know? The same as any shifter pack."

Huh. That wasn't much to go on.

We fell into silence for a few more miles until eventually, Reid spoke up again.

"You know Naomi, right? She's one of the Thornwood Clan. Or used to be, anyway." He shrugged. "Who knows where she's at, these days."

I wrinkled my nose. Of course, I knew Naomi. My brother's on-again, off-again ex. In the old days, she'd stick around just long enough to mark her territory and get Jason hooked on her before prancing off again. She reminded me of a poisonous flower: lovely to look at, but you didn't want to get too close.

When Tammy had entered the picture, I wasn't the only one in the clan to breathe a sigh of relief. Naomi had scampered away. I didn't know where she was, and frankly, I didn't care.

Reid caught my frown and broke into laughter. "Aw, c'mon! You can't judge a whole clan by one wolf, Kara."

I made a noise and crossed my arms. "Fine. What about the others? The old Alpha had a son, right?"

"Uh, yeah." Reid shifted in his seat. "Two of 'em. I've only met the younger one, though. Kit Thornwood."

"What's he like?" I pressed.

"He's cool."

Ugh. I would get so much more out of Allara.

I couldn't tell if Reid was holding back on me for some reason, or if he genuinely didn't have any other information to share.

My shifter senses were on high alert. The farther we drove from the village, the edgier I became. The wolf in me was wary as all hell. Every bump in the road made me flinch back in my seat.

If I'm heading into an unknown, I'd rather go in with my eyes open.

But I didn't bother trying to pry any further, I would just find out when I arrived.